Likely Plays a Joker

As a young man Malcolm Noble served in the Portsmouth police, a chapter in his life that provides some background to his crime fiction. He has written fourteen mystery novels set in the south of England from the 1920s to the 1960s. He has presented his own weekly book programme on local radio and has had two plays produced on fm radio. Press reviews have emphasised his sense of place and atmosphere, his strong characterisation and first rate storytelling.

Malcolm Noble now lives in Market Harborough where he and his wife run a second-hand bookshop.

Malcolm Noble's Crime Fiction

"Suspenseful, darkly funny and beautifully written."

(Historical Novels Society)

"The books feature a host of interesting and unusual characters as well as a well defined sense of time and place."
(John Martin/Crime Scene Britain and Ireland: A Reader's Guide

"Good fun and a fast enjoyable read."
(Shropshire Star)

"Noble has a fine knack of description, creating a sense of place and atmosphere. Try them."

(Portsmouth Post)

"A dead good read. A mesmerising murder mystery."

(Harborough Mail)

"A marvellous creation. Noble reels off a first rate story. Vastly entertaining. Noble makes good use of his knowledge of the world of crime."
(Nottingham Post)

"A great success. Very talented writing skills."
(102.3 Harboroughfm)

"An original, absorbing and compulsive read for all fans of this genre."
(Telford and Wrekin Advertiser)

"This fantastic new novel. It leaves you begging for the next in the series."
(Montgomeryshire Advertiser)

"This is parochial policing at its best."
(Shropshire Star)

"If you like your murder mysteries, these books are for you."
(BBC Leics)

Mystery novels by the same author

Peggy Pinch Investigates
Peggy Pinch, Policeman's Wife
Murder in a Parish Chest
The Body in the Bicycle Shed

The Timberdick Mysteries
A Mystery of Cross Women
The Case of the Dirty Verger
Timberdick's First Case
Liking Good Jazz
Piggy Tucker's Poison
The Parish of Frayed Ends
The Clue of the Curate's Cushion
The Case of the Naughty Wife
The Poisons of Goodladies Road
Take Seven Cooks (a play)

The Ned Machray Memoirs
The Baker Street Protectors

"Parochial Policing at its Best" *(Shropshire Star)*
malcolmnoble.com

Malcolm Noble

Likely Plays a Joker
Detective Inspector 'Likely' Storey

The Crime Stock
2016

*Published for the Crime Stock by the Bookcabin Press
7-9 Coventry Road, Market Harborough LE16 9BX*

Likely Plays a Joker

*Copyright © 2016 Malcolm Noble
The moral right of the author has been asserted.*

Apart from fair dealing for the purposes of research or private study, or criticism or review, permitted under the Copyright, Designs and Patents Act 1988, this publication may only be reproduced, stored or transmitted, in any form or means, with the prior permission in writing of the publisher, or in the case of reprographic reproduction in accordance with the terms of licences issued by the Copyright Licensing Agency. Enquiries concerning reproduction outside those terms should be sent to the publishers.

This is a work of fiction. All persons and events are imaginary and any resemblance to actual persons and events is purely coincidental.

7 6 5 4 3 2 **1**

ISBN 978-0-9932700-7-9

To Christine

Relying on the excuse that credibility is more important than authenticity, I can lightly confess to occasionally stretching the boundaries of history.

My most obvious offence is delaying Eden's resignation as Foreign Secretary by one week. My diligent reader will also notice that the wireless programmes are typical rather than accurate. The number of vehicles available to my small borough force is not unrealistic if we agree that it seems to have been a well resourced constabulary for the period. I hope that these liberties do not spoil the story.

Followers of my crime fiction will say that they recognise the town that inspired the setting of my totally fictitious tale. But, please, it was no more than a starting point. You will not recognise the geography, the people or the pubs.

Malcolm Noble
malcolmnoble.com

Part One

Chapter One

Detective Inspector Brian 'Likely' Storey of the Borough Police struck a redheaded match from his box of Captain Webbs and laid the truculent flame over the bowl of his workaday pipe. He said between puffs, "And you walked through a brick wall?"

Her name was Edith Winterton but he had decided to think of her as Snoozy Snowflake. A woman who would drift wherever the outside wind took her. She was well turned out and by no means silly but she was nervous, shivery and ready to weep. There wasn't a hint of make believe on her face.

"Definitely. I simply stepped forward and found myself on the other side."

"The other side might have curious connotations in this case. You mean the first floor landing?"

"Are you laughing at me, inspector?"

"Not at all."

"Do you think I'm mad?"

"If I did, I still wouldn't laugh at you." The pipe didn't want to light that morning. He took it from his mouth and looked sideways at the hand carved relief around the bowl. He never trusted fancy pipes but Janine insisted that he deserved something particular whenever she bought a present. He stuck the stem between his teeth; he'd give it another go in a few minutes. "No, I don't think you're mad, Edith."

"But you don't believe me?"

Storey pushed himself back in the upholstered armchair and breathed in to ease the strain on the buttons of his waistcoat. Piles of books and documents had been on his desk for weeks -

months maybe, who could remember? Two phones, his tray of pens and his photographs of Janine and her girls sat on the books, and leaves of old notepaper poked out from the stacks. (Desks in the investigations room, beyond the heavy panelled door of his office, were much the same except that they had extra phones. Two weeks ago, even more phones had been connected which had to stand on pedestals. It was nonsense.) He said, "I have a young constable. Harry. He's a very promising lad; my sergeant has great hopes for him. He visited 18 Coldwater Place, this morning, and I have his report here." He pinched a page of the boy's scribbled notes between his thumb and finger. "I congratulate you, Edith, on an accurate and detailed description. Harry found it just as you reported to us except, that is, for the grey haired tortoise, the bulb nosed gnome and the black-hooded crow."

"I didn't say that I saw the creatures, inspector, only that the voice spoke of them."

He poked at the tobacco in the pipe bowl with the stub end of a match. "Are you cold in here, Edith? It's very warm, believe me. I have the cleaners make up the fire, ninety minutes before I'm due each morning. I think you'd better tell me again about the voice."

"He started by saying, 'Come into the unknown.' "

Storey smiled and cursed himself for it. It wouldn't take much to discourage the woman and then he would learn nothing.

She said, "That's when he mentioned the grey haired tortoise, the bulb nosed gnome and the black-hooded crow who speaks with the voice of three old women at the same time. He called it the unknown room of the grey haired tortoise. He told me to look into the burning coals."

"The coals in the fire?"

"Yes, inspector, and that's where I would find the jewel, the Red Fire of the East. Inspector Storey, I said straightaway 'There is no one in this room.' I said, 'Where are you speaking from?' But he wouldn't answer. He insisted that I should kneel at the hearth and stare through the flames. He said, 'Tell me that the jewel-fire does not burn red, like the moon alight.' Then the other voices..."

"The voices of three women who spoke as one?"

"You remember the words, yes, just as I've told you. 'Reach for the jewel,' they said. 'Put your fingers through the flames and take it for yourself.' I'm not stupid, inspector. I said that I wouldn't, that I'd been tricked into coming to the room. But they kept saying, 'Do it, Edie. So easy. Reach out. The spirits will protect you. Do it, Edie. Do it.' I'm sorry. I'm imitating the voices."

"Of course. I expect you to." He was trying a second match over his pipe. "You burnt yourself?"

"Yes."

"So, the fire was real."

"That's when it got really frightening. Till then, I'd been no more than scared."

"Nervous, yes."

" 'You see! Each time your fingers probe forward, the jewel fire retreats.' "

"This was the three women?"

"No. The man's voice. He said that the Red Fire of the East can only be taken when a girl steps into the fire. 'Step through the flames.' He'd become very insistent."

"As you suggest, things had taken a dangerous turn."

"The women warned me. 'Once through, you can't come back. Be sure, Edie. Be sure in what you do.' I shouted that I wanted to get out. I wanted to leave."

"And they told you to walk through the wall? Please, I know you can remember the exact words."

"The exact words? 'The doors and windows are locked from the outside but you are free to leave. If you believe everything you have seen in this room, you will be able to walk through the walls.' I went crazy at them. This is nonsense, I shouted. Some sort of trick. There must be hidden speakers, wires and echoes.

"Oh yes, gov."

"... all these experiences have left a residue. Do you know what it is?"

The mantelpiece clock struck the half hour, too quietly for the inspector to notice. If Faulkner could divert the old man into telling the story of how he had stolen the clock from the old training school, he might stall this case in its tracks. Instead, he admitted sorrowfully, "The itch."

"An itch, Faulkner, an itch between the backs of my shoulders whenever I'm likely to discard some simple fact, some hint, no more than a less experienced investigator would rightly dismiss and yet ... "

"Why did she go to the house in the first place?"

The inspector confessed, "I never got to the bottom of that."

"Governor, you asked for my thoughts. I have had to send Haynes and St John back to uniform. We'll see no hair of them before Easter which means we won't be able to keep a proper watch on the Knights Street jewellers. Young Harry is putting together the court file for the Kitts prosecution and he's three days behind. He wants to come in tomorrow, Sunday, but I've told him no. Me, I am trying to get three different uniform teams to understand the meaning of diligent patrols and you, governor, you have to chair a review this afternoon. You remember, the Poynton Tribunal."

Storey made up his mind. "Harry!" He was ready to stand up again and wrestled like an infant tied to his chair. "There is something about this case, Faulkner. It feels ... beyond time."

"Yes, gov."

Storey recognised the weary frustration on Faulkner's face. "Yes," he said, "it's not easy being my sergeant. No doubt, you put up with jokes, comments ... digs. Do you get many digs? I guess so. People say that your detective inspector is a duffer, promoted because he is an old boy, but tucked away in an office where he can do no harm. A quiet borough force suits him well, old 'Likely'. He can chair the Poynton Review with council officials and we'll ignore whatever he reports. You see, 'Likely' was all right as a Number Two, a deputy. Huh, not even a deputy. Let's say a sidekick. He doesn't like people, that's the trouble with Likely." He mimicked, "He can't get on wi' folk."

"Governor, I didn't mean ..."

"This is good coffee. Are we shopping somewhere new?" He tried to relax and found himself gazing at the family photograph. "I need unusual things to do, sergeant. And this case has one undeniable fact which must surely be denied. All sense says it must be denied. Faulkner, that woman is convinced that she walked through a brick wall. That makes it a case worthy of the best detectives in England."

My God, it was stifling in the office. Faulkner had never known his inspector open a window and if the door remained shut for more than ten minutes, the heat from the coal fire made a suet crust of everything.

Only the door broke young Harry's rush to the office. "You wanted me, gov?"

"What's that in your hand?"

"A crust, gov. Sorry."

"Come in, come in. Are you sure there were no pictures of grey haired tortoises in Coldwater Place?"

"I checked, gov." The fledgling detective stood on a tattered rug which he had come to regard as his own. Only once, when he had first joined the team, had he been invited to sit as the inspector interviewed him. Ever since, his place had been to stand.

"What is a grey haired tortoise?" Storey asked deliberately.

"I can't imagine, gov."

"I can't picture one," added Faulkner.

"Curious, don't you both think? I mean, a curious fantasy. No one else would think of it. Try this one; a black hooded crow?"

"A raven?" Harry suggested.

Storey nodded. "Bulb nosed goblin?"

17

"Plasticine," said Faulkner, without adding that the whole thing was nonsense.

"No, no. It's the Red Fire of the East that's the key. What is the desk sergeant at Willow Place doing? He's good at this sort of thing?"

"He's the Head Constable's choice for the hospital project."

Storey mouthed the words silently, then asked, "What is a hospital project? Send him to the public library in North Street. He's to bury himself in books. I want to know what this jewel is all about."

Faulkner pressed, "Governor, can we think this through?" He would have gone further but for the youngster's presence.

"Harry, drop what you're doing."

Faulkner groaned.

"I want you to watch Coldwater Place. If Edith Winterton turns up, get as close as you can without giving the game away. Of you go, lad."

"Yes, gov."

The junior's eager exit left a quietness in the office that was uncomfortable for both men. Storey had learned that the patience of others behaved like bank accounts. Without nourishment, they naturally favoured emptiness. Any inspector needed to keep his sergeant on his side. "I remember the Fleming Park case, Faulkner. It started like this. Yes, very much like this. I was working for Evanshaw at the time so there was little time for gossip, but Sergeant Gilbert and I managed to get a lunch in the Pegasus and came across an old cracksman called Brown. Billy Brown. What time is it? Lord, it's a quarter to one. Come on, sergeant, we've time for lunch. Lunch is important."

This meeting of the Poynton Committee was worse than any that Storey could remember. He doodled on his notepad. He had completed the front half of a grey haired tortoise when he purposely stubbed the pencil, breaking its lead. There's no such animal, he told himself, and because Edith had not seen one, it could not exist even in her imagination. Without excusing himself, he abandoned his chair and, using a telephone in the corridor, enquired if the Willow Place sergeant had discovered anything during his research. History had recorded nothing about the Red Fire of the East, it seemed.

Storey extended his intermission with a drink of water at the top of the staircase. Three flights down, one of the women was trying to stow a bucket and mop in a cupboard. Two voices he didn't recognise were arguing about the new 999 system. "Don't bring that mongrel in here!" bawled a sergeant on the ground floor.

The creatures and gremlins were no more than hearsay evidence. The voice could have been -and probably was- the girl's imagination. But no one could imagine that they had walked through a wall, surely? How would some scoundrel convince a sensible woman that she had done that?

When he sat down again at the head of the table, a cocked eyebrow indicated that the man from Highways and Bridges, seated to his left, had noticed the nude Edith Winterton riding the tortoise across the top page of Storey's pad. He called for the next item on the agenda and began to lightly pencil some clothes on the skinny form.

Now, people were agreeing with the man who was speaking. How could he talk such inconsequential clap-trap? And how could others agree with him?

He looked up and, although he didn't speak at first, the discussion faltered in mid-sentence. "Has anyone been outside?" he asked. "I could manage only a coffee and roll in the canteen, but has anyone looked at the weather?" He stopped the murmurings with a rap on the table edge. "I mean, is it dusty out there? Does it get to your throat, this afternoon?" Then more precisely, "Would anyone feel poorly walking in it."

The man from Highways was eager to respond. He adjusted his glasses, he straightened his tie -- but he couldn't think of anything to say. The rest of the committee were nonplussed by the inspector's outburst. One wrote, 'It goes to show,' on a slip of paper and passed it around, neighbour to neighbour. The looks on their faces made it clear that the committee wouldn't need to put up with such outbursts if a county man was in the chair.

Later, when the meeting had broken up and Storey was out of the way, the man from Highways and Bridges spoke up for him. "He's an eccentric. He brings different thinking." But he was battling against the tide. The lady from National Rivers gained a ripple of applause for her lyrical yet dogged succinctness. "It is unsafe that the town's investigation of crime - Lord forbid murder - should be in the hands of an unstable old carthorse."

The next morning, when he was sure that the hot sandwiches had arrived from the canteen, that the coffee was hot in its pot and the team were ready to discuss their day's business, Storey folded the woman's letter, returned it to its envelope and tucked it out of sight. He walked out of his office to join his men.

"You look excited, Harry," he said placidly. He checked that the sergeant had locked the door so that they wouldn't be disturbed and he gave the look that reminded them not to fiddle with their work during their chat. They had placed a chair for the inspector in the middle of the room; the others sat at their desks.

"Sergeant Faulkner was right," said Harry. "No one went in or out during the evening and I was ready to think that we had been wasting my time. But then, the woman turned up at five minutes to twelve. I made sure she didn't see me."

"Ah, five minutes to midnight. D. I. Evanshaw had some interesting thoughts about five minutes to midnight. This was, ooh, twenty or twenty five years ago. He said that twelve o'clock was like a plate of glass that everyone knew would be breached but some onlookers found the tension so great that, at five to midnight, they were likely to break it themselves, simply to relieve the tension. His point, gentlemen, was that people act irrationally at five minutes to midnight." He was about to bring his pipe from his coat when he noticed the toasted sandwich on the corner of what had been, until yesterday, Constable St John's desk. "Sausage," he enquired, "with OK Sauce?"

"From your personal bottle, gov," Faulkner confirmed.

"You continued your observations, Harry?"

"Better than that. I went up to Coldwater Place and Dorothy Langworthy invited me in."

"She's got a face like a sun dried newt, you say?"

"I think it's worse. There was nothing unusual in there. Nothing was going on, governor. Our woman wasn't there. There were no other visitors. But I insisted that we shared a pot of tea. I wasn't going to be fobbed off."

Faulkner offered: "It didn't occur to you that you had been drawn indoors so that you wouldn't see what was happening outside?"

Harry looked around the room.

"Fortunately, nothing was happening outside," said Storey. "You discontinued your observations?"

"I telephoned Sergeant Faulkner at twenty past four and he gave me permission to leave, gov."

"Twenty past four? You stood there from midnight until four o'clock?"

"But I didn't go straight home. I checked out that home address she had given us and it's completely false. No one knows anything about Snoozy Snowflake at number 239 on the Denning Flats." P.C. Harry was embarrassed. His inspector had chosen the nickname and it wasn't to be appropriated.

Storey asked mildly, "And at what time did you make these enquiries?"

"A quarter to five, sir."

"People were happy about that?"

"Not over much," Harry conceded. "There was a bit of knocking on walls and rattling of windows. You know how it is when you wake people up. A woman on the opposite balcony kept shouting that it was a police raid and I couldn't shut her up."

Storey's little finger dabbed the last of the brown sauce from the corners of his mouth. "I have received a letter. In a moment I will share it with you." He finished his mouthful, replaced the empty saucer on the corner of St John's desk, and washed his mouth with a good swallow of the dark coffee. Then he opened the envelope. "My dear police inspector. By the time you read this letter, I shall have passed over to the other side. You will find nothing wrong at Coldwater Place and people will not have heard of me at my home address. I might never have existed and you will find no mystery to solve."

"Very concerning," Faulkner said grimly.

"But fortunately our Head Constable has assured me that all is well. The letter, he says, is flim-flam. He wanted to know why I was wasting my time on fairy-tales and pantomime. We have no missing person enquiry, no case of abduction and no murder. I find this comforting. However, he was cross that I had removed his sergeant from the great hospital venture and he wanted to know why I had withdrawn the observations of the Knights Road jewellers. He suggested that my department needed greater supervision. I put him right on that last point." Storey was holding his coffee cup in one hand and the saucer in the other. For no reason, he turned the saucer upside down so that he could read the potter's mark. A morsel of coffee dripped onto his trouser leg. He inhaled deeply through his nose. "Otherwise, I agree with our Head Constable's judgement. I have been the butt of a hoax. A joke. But I would still like to know why."

Chapter Two

Frost on a sunny morning, Monday 27 February, reminded Likely of early Easter Holidays. No doubt, there had been only a few sunny frosts but, as he dawdled through the *Daily Sketch* (Janine's choice) at the breakfast table, he was happy to recall nippy bicycle rides through the country lanes of his childhood. "I shall walk into work this morning."

Janine was making their bed. She shouted through, "You need to leave now if you're not going to be late."

He shifted the marmalade and turned a page. "No, I shall leave when I'm ready and I shall be deliberately late." He lifted his face. "Can you be deliberately late? Surely, if you arrive when you mean to, you're on time. I'll take a detour through the Malster Estate. I used to enjoy patrolling that beat on early shifts when I first joined. I saw my first arrest on the Malster. Have I told you that?"

"Yes, dear."

"There were fewer cars, of course."

"And not so many houses. It's quite an ugly place now."

"Certainly, the parks were larger."

Janine poked her head through the door, attractively holding her figure against the frame. "You could take the morning off and we could go shopping. That would be nice."

"Yes." He considered the attractive prospect of taking morning coffee with her in Dickins and Jones, overlooking their friendly High Street where traditional shopkeepers stood in doorways and familiar figures swapped stories on the pavement. If he hadn't a conscience about the extra work that Faulkner had been putting in, he might not have retracted his promise. "No," he said. "I've things to clear up."

Saturday's story, featuring the spiritual Miss 'Snowflake' had melted away; it could have been a week away. Harry, having completed his court file, had been pinched by the motor patrol with a brief to deter bicycle thefts on the remote edges of the city. Faulkner confined himself to his desk with no hope of parole until the backlog of dried up cases had been signed off. This craze for bringing things to order had gingered up Storey to do something with the mess in his office. Hence, his idea of turning up late.

The desk sergeant at central, famous for shaving his bald head twice a day, caught him as he approached the foyer lifts. "Likely! I didn't mean to get you into trouble."

Storey stopped, turned slowly and approached the counter. Sergeant Miller was obstreperous, cocksure and thought he was fire proof. Rumours had placed him at that corner table in the Grayling where fascist thinkers talked through long evenings (but Storey had watched and found nothing to report.) The regulator posted him, mischievously, at the front desk because he knew that Miller had no patience with the public.

Storey kept his voice low. "My name is Detective Inspector Storey. You can call me Mr Storey or Inspector Storey or, conveniently, inspector. You can try gov, and if I don't think you're being impertinent, I shan't jab you in your eye with this pipe stem. Nobody calls me Likely to my face."

The sergeant had difficulty taking that. He said, not meaning it, "I'm sorry, sir. I wanted to apologise before you heard it from anyone else. That's all."

So, Sergeant Miller knew something that Storey didn't. Their eyes were locked for a few seconds.

"You've some news?"

"They've found a woman with her belly ripped out, across the canal from Coldwater Place. I recognised the description and had to tell them that she'd called at your office on Saturday. They reckon she's been dead long enough to make it a murder during that night."

Storey went on looking, impassively, suddenly aware of the weight of the coat, jacket and scarf on his shoulders.

"Skelton's opened a murder room on county's top floor, and the Head Constable's been in since seven."

"Thank you. You were right to interrupt me." He nodded once. "Thank you, sergeant."

As he rode alone in the lift, he kept his hands in his coat pockets and turned the pipe between his fingers. 'Across the canal' meant that the body was within county's jurisdiction. He pouted (something he did only when he was alone). Even if she had been found on the borough's side of the boundary, Skelton would have been brought in. Storey's name had been taken off the list of detectives that could be assigned to murders some years ago.

Faulkner had already been alerted of his governor's arrival and was making coffee at the little refreshment table in the corner of the detectives' room. He was wearing the best jacket which he always kept in the cupboard, in case of important visitors.

"He's in your office." He was searching for the tray with the white napkin.

"You left it at the bottom of my glass cabinet. Use the ordinary one."

"I couldn't stop him, governor. He's opened your window."

The Head Constable of the Borough (they didn't have chiefs in towns like this) was immaculate from the top of his precisely trimmed hair to his starched collar, expensive suit and waxed shoe laces. Storey always admired gentlemen who could master the knack of keeping their trousers legs at the right length. The turn-ups of the charcoal suit touched the instep of the Head's shoes without resting on them.

"Skelton will want to talk with you."

"Of course, and I can let him have Harry's report of his observations on Coldwater Place."

"He has already seconded the lad to his investigation."

"Mr Skelton mustn't confuse things. Harry is a witness in the case. But it's no problem." The two men began to negotiate their way around the cramped office, accepting that they would neither sit down, stand still nor get in each other's way. "I would like to continue one or two enquiries of my own," Storey said. "Her visit here was a hoax. Someone was playing a joke on me but I'm rather impressed, sir. It was an elaborate and carefully thought out prank. I'm interested in that false address she gave us."

"We were hoping you would take that line. I spoke to the Watch Chair before breakfast. Sir Jason has taken over from Donohue." They were no more than names to Storey. Even if he recognised either man, he would have had no time for them. "But you report directly and without fail to me, Likely. We can't tolerate crossed lines. We live in difficult times."

"Crossed lines would be regrettable."

Faulkner knocked on the door. Storey waited for his superior to answer. When his superior didn't call the sergeant to enter, Storey kept quiet too and Faulkner went away.

Now, the Head Constable brought a toffee-nosed edge to his voice. "We were wondering if you are best employed in these poky offices. We were thinking, you're one of our most experienced investigators."

"I have worked with some of the best detectives in England."

"Dodridge of B Division. That must have been an intriguing experience. Sharp, Dodridge was. Very sharp."

"And Dowding, of course. Evanshaw, Benny Graythorpe."

"And that man in the Fahrenheit Case."

"Hampton, sir, Hampton of the Fahrenheit Case. However, I am very contented in these poky offices. I'm not part of any hierarchy and the borough is good enough to pass some interesting cases across our desks. The council panels are a bugbear. Their natural state is do-nothing."

The Head nodded. "Inertia." He turned his back and looked out of the window, so Storey sat in the visitor's easy chair.

"The question, Likely, is that we're not sure we can justify your sergeant and a constable. It's hardly fair on them."

"You mean, working for Likely Storey is unlikely to earn points for promotion."

"That's partly it. Well, the greater part of it." He was playing with the window's sash. "When this murder is done with, young Harry will return to the motor patrol. You keep your sergeant."

Storey's response was to draw his pipe from his pocket and light up; something he would not normally do in the Head Constable's presence.

"We will be sending you a Boy Scout."

He took the pipe from between his teeth and queried mildly, "A Boy Scout?"

"Not a real one."

"Oh good. Only a pretend one."

"Storey, our borough receives many requests to join from under age applicants. We could turn them away, I know."

"Don't we usually employ them as civilians until they're twenty one?"

"Sir Jason has in mind something more promising. The Watch Committee has agreed to a new post, one of Clerk Cadet. But we wouldn't expect them to be tethered to deskwork. No, we should prepare them for service in a more purposeful way."

"Yes, I can see that has more promise. How many will we need?"

"Oh, one at a time, Storey. Good lord, only one."

"I see. You want me to take one of these 'Boy Scouts' and beef them up for the selection interview."

"Quite so, Storey. You have the idea."

Twenty minutes later, Storey stormed from his office. "I've been butchered, Faulkner, and I don't like it. I'm off to do some detective work." He was half way through the door when he leaned back with the instruction, "Do not let anybody in!"

"No, gov."

It was three o'clock and all serious business had been done in the shambles. Traders were waiting to take down their displays and any last minute shopper had to put up with the inattention of hands who wanted to go home. He found the tiled staircase to the flats above and had to interrupt a children's ball game before he could get to the top landing. The concrete beneath his feet was wet where folk had washed patches at their front doors but the water had nowhere to go. Washing hung on lines stretched from balconies and guttering. A fat pensioner in a vest leaned over the railing and shouted at the women on the roadway, "Eden's gone!" He'd left his door open and a radio squawked from his home. It was unusual for the B.B.C. to broadcast news before six so Storey understood not that some heavenly garden had disappeared but that the Foreign Secretary had resigned.

He kept up a steady pace; he didn't pause as he lit his pipe to mask the smells of raw meat and cheap disinfectant. He decided that life in the Denning Flats was one long toil to keep clean against the odds.

He thought he had reached the right corner of the landing and brought out the photo of Edith which had been circulated and Harry's slip of paper with her address. A woman, carrying coal in a shopping basket, wanted him to get out of her way. "What're you needin', grandpa?" Then, with no prompting, she nodded at the photograph. "She's usually in the Red Rose cafe on Mondays from two. Try, but you won't find her in."

"I'm not sure which door to knock."

She plodded past him. "One with her number on it would be a good one to start with."

Accepting her advice with good grace, the detective knocked, knocked again and pushed against the door. He looked over his shoulder. Because no one was looking, he braced his shoulder and barged against the woodwork.

"Easy enough," squeaked a young voice, already stretched with the Denning Placade accent. "But you'll have to fix it afterwards. You should try the twist and squeeze trick."

A young citizen was behind Storey's left knee. He was leaning over the handlebar of his tricycle, eighteen inches from the ground. He had odd sandals, a cut down shirt and, because his mother could give him no underpants, a corner of brown paper protruded from his shorts.

"Here, let Thomas show you." He dismounted, produced a steel comb from his waistband, completed the twist and squeeze method and, with a light touch, pushed the front door open. The detective inspector watched the infant return to his trike. He bowed his head and quietly said thank you.

He kept his hands in his coat pockets so that he wouldn't touch anything accidentally. The Denning was within the borough boundary but Skelton was leading the investigation so this was Skelton's territory. The place should have been busy with fingerprint officers and cameramen with a clutch of detectives waiting for the go ahead to search every drawer and cupboard. No doubt, the investigator had accepted Harry's conclusion that the Snowflake woman had given a false address but, standing on the worn carpet of her sitting-room, Storey realised that Harry had ventured no further than the front door. Here, the detective inspector could taste Snowflake's history with the place. He recognised the smell of her cheap scent and the hairdressing she used. When she had visited his office, she moved her chair to the same angle that this chair met the hearthrug. The light from the windows bothered her, he guessed.

Her flat comprised the sitting-room, bedroom and kitchen. Storey had to search hard for the bathroom; it was no more than a cupboard annexed to the kitchen. The bedroom was neat. He didn't bother with it. He wasn't here to do a thorough search. Instead, he spent time in the kitchen, trying to learn as much as he could about the dead woman. Had she been a sugar or salt person, fat or fruit, boiled or fried?

Back in the sitter, he noticed the photograph of her mother and father. He guessed their ages and the age of the picture and worked out that they would both be dead by now. (He warmed to the idea of Skelton wasting days trying to find them.) Two letters were propped on the mantelpiece. He did not want to finger them so he brought a pair of scissors, knife and a fork from the kitchen and, by practised and careful engineering, managed to extricate the pages from the envelopes. They were from friends - Storey noted their names and addresses - and the second letter offered the clue that Storey was hoping for. Snowflake had a lover called Bob.

It was an honest home with no hint that Snowflake lost herself in daydreams or imagination. There wasn't a film star or story paper in the place. He sighed, a little frustrated. So far, only common sense said that she had been making things up. Everything else said that she was a genuine and sensible woman.

He left Number 239 as he had found it and retraced his steps. As he came out of the shambles and into the street, the tower clock stuck four o'clock. He was pleased that his enquiries in the flats had yielded more than he had expected but he was still smarting over the demolition of his department. Boy Scouts? He might as well call his office a home for waifs and strays. He decided to spend an hour where no one would know where to find him. It was his little way of punishing them.

The Red Rose restaurant, ten minutes walk from the Denning Flats, was squashed between an old fashioned barbershop and an ironmongery with too many buckets on the pavement. This was one of the main roads out of the city and, because most of the traffic was haulage, it was choked by fumes from old growlers. The grime stuck to windows and, in the evenings, turned the streetlights to musty amber. It wasn't unusual to witness a cyclist give up the fight and wheel his bike along the pavements rather than breathe in the waste from the lorries. This trunk road had the crossroads which were governed by the earliest traffic lights in the city. Storey could remember how, just three years ago, families had come here to watch the stopping and starting and schoolboys soon became expert on the timings and sequence. For that first season, an afternoon at the crossroads had been as good as a couple of hours train spotting.

He chose a table at the window and ordered a pot of tea with a slice of cake.

"Butter with your cake?" asked the young girl in a white pinny

"No thank you."

She was scribbling on her pad. "You've got to have butter. It's complimentary." (She said, 'couple-a-mentary'.)

Storey counted eight tables and forty seats (he couldn't stop himself collecting information) but he was the only customer.

The proprietor, perspiring his in collarless shirt and a stained apron tied around his waist, arrived with his tea tray which he set on a corner table. "Over here if you like, chief inspector."

"You mean you don't want a policeman at the window?"

"It will discourage others who might be thinking of coming in."

"I'm surprised you recognised me. Your name?"

"Williams." Now he was dusting the table cloth.

"Well, Mr Williams. I am staying at the table I have chosen. I ordered cake with my tea but I think I will also take a dish of pie and custard. Please, leave the cake. I can crumble it into the custard. I'm sorry, it's a childish habit of mine." Storey's pipe came out of his pocket. "No, no," he insisted as he leaned back to search for his tobacco pouch, straining his waistcoat buttons. "Before you go, tell me how you recognised my face."

"Because a young piece showed me your photograph two, three weeks ago maybe. She wanted to know who you were. I said I didn't know but the face was of an ugly old bugger and if I'd ever met him, I'd never forget him."

Storey thought, Edith Winterton had never been a young piece, even in the olden days.

"Two days later, she's in here again and says you're a chief inspector from central but she doesn't know your name." He picked up the empty tray. "Neither do I and I don't want to. I'll fetch your custard."

"It's 'inspector' by the way. We don't have chiefs in the borough."

He easily pictured Snowflake coming to this cafe. She would have enjoyed sitting by the far wall, watching the comings and goings. Would she have occupied herself with a crossword? No, not a crossword, he thought, but certainly a simpler puzzle. She'd like patterns. Yes, she'd like to draw patterns. But why on Monday afternoons? Not that Monday afternoons were suspicious, but they were part of her life that he needed to understand.

The pretty waitress in her pinny had been told to stand on a stool and polish the windows. Sure enough, her stretching and reaching enticed a couple of business gentlemen with umbrellas. They organised themselves at the table Storey had, in his head, chosen for Snowflake and began to talk louder than they needed to. It was obvious that they hoped to chat with the waitress when she arrived to take their order.

Storey could see through a curtain to the back of the restaurant, where Williams was instructing the girl in ways to encourage a larger order than the pair meant to spend.

When he returned with pie and custard, and a tiny pot of cream on the house, Storey asked about the girl with the photograph.

"Was she a regular customer?"

"Apart from that twice, never been in before or since."

"So why, Mr Williams? Why did she have a picture of me and want to know my name?"

"I'll give you benefits from my thoughts, because I have been thinking about this. You see, unusual." He made the most of the word, exaggerating the movement of his lips. "Decent people, they don't know policemen by names. Most of them wouldn't know a copper unless they were local to his beat and he wasn't above sergeant. So, do you know what I think? I think someone had told her to trust you." He tapped his knuckle on the table cloth. "Five foot ten or eleven but looks taller in her heels. Black hair, long and rolling like the women on the pictures. Slim, good little bottom that she'd like to wiggle, given the chance. Enjoy your custard."

Chapter Three

"It's five o'clock," Storey announced when he swept into the office. As he was taking off his hat, he noticed a young woman sitting beneath the hat stand so he turned the gesture into a polite bow of his head. He kept moving, "Follow me, Sergeant Faulkner. We've made progress."

Faulkner wanted to make coffee first. He remembered that his governor had said that he liked the new brand, and he needed to be well looked after before he heard the news. But Storey was calling insistently.

The first thing Faulkner said was, "The Boy Scout has arrived, governor."

Storey, seated behind the chaos of his desk, looked up and froze. "Sergeant, how long have we known each other? We've talked before. I think we said 1921. A little shy of seventeen years. Of course, we have not worked together throughout that age but you know me well, Faulkner. You know that I have worked with the best detectives in England."

"Yes, gov."

Still, Storey's head did not move. "There is no need to list them. We know them. Dowding. Evanshaw. Dodridge of B Division. Why, only this morning our Head Constable was reminding me how impressed he was with Dodridge. There's no need to mention the others. Graythorpe, of course."

Faulkner bid for time. "Hampton of the Fahrenheit Case."

"Indeed, there was Hampton of the Fahrenheit Case." He relaxed enough to tap his fingertips on his inky blotter. "You've been there at my failures, let's be frank, and even now a day

34

does not pass when you don't cover for me. I've always thought that you know me, good and proper, thoroughly. That's why I asked you to join the team. I was looking for a sergeant who would know when to push and when not to go too far. Most of all, you understand my sense of humour. I do have a sense of humour, sergeant."

"Indeed, governor."

"You know what I find funny and what I find misplaced." He rose to his feet and pressed his knuckles on the desk top. "You know that I do not find talk of women, funny talk." He leaned forward as his voice rose. "Do not tell me," he pointed a finger at the door and shouted: "that the woman under the hats is our Boy Scout!"

His roar carried along the corridor and into offices. Young clerks giggled and telephoned their colleagues. Sergeant Miller, seated in his favourite stall in the gents, kept his balance only by holding on. The Head Constable's clerk was ready to laugh but she was half way up the staircase with both arms weighed down by piles of documents, so she didn't risk it. The ladies in the canteen suggested sending down some extra raspberry tart (there was no mistaking Storey's voice) while Sir Jason, the Chairman of the Borough Watch Committee making use of their own select with its library, cocktail cabinet and the discreet supply of quality stationery, looked up from his treatise on Roman law and smiled, "Ah, Storey has heard the good news."

The intended prey stood up from her perch beneath the hat stand and stepped uncertainly towards the lion's den. Sir Jason had assured her that D.I. Likely's bark was worse than his bite but, right now, she attached little confidence to that. She clutched the doorknob and pushed her way in. "Excuse me, chief," she said. (She knew it sounded timid, but the roar had been a very loud roar.)

"One! Always knock on my door. Two! Having knocked, wait for an invitation. Three! When invited, you count to five, allowing me plenty of time to be ready." He was on his feet, holding onto the desk as his rage swayed him backwards and forwards. "What do you want?"

She advanced. Five feet four, he thought, she's a fighter, light on her feet and quick with her fists. She had a spring in her step as if she were ready to jump and didn't care if the fall would be too great. She had tied her dirt coloured hair back and tucked it in, trying to match the conventions of a police station. He decided, a quick thinker and smart with it.

"I would like to tell my uncle," she was saying, "that the head detective has made me especially welcome, that I'm already part of the team and, in fact, I've got that quite at home feeling."

Storey kept his mouth closed and allowed a groan to vibrate in his throat like some ritual mating call. Faulkner closed his eyes; she had chosen the worst possible approach.

"It is, you're right, quite wrong of me to use his name but your opening salvo, chief, frankly, it's scared the pants off me and I need all the ammunition I can get."

He wanted her out of his office. "Do you want anything else?"

Faulkner tried to warn her with a shake of his head.

"When Sir Jason interviewed me (it wasn't really an interview, it was a tete-a-tete over tea by the river) my wish was to work with the best detectives in England."

Storey could feel the words bubbling on his lips. "Get her out of here, Faulkner, while I phone the Head Constable and let him know what I've been up to."

The girl was already on her way. Faulkner got as far as the door, then made matters plain. "Before you telephone H.C., we will share a coffee and a pipe. I'll bring in my special twenty minute briar and we can talk."

Storey nodded. Calmly, he asked, "Did she really say, 'scared the pants off me' and must she call me chief? It makes me feel like a New York cop."

Her name was Deborah H. Holden. She was laying a clean napkin over the tray and waiting for the kettle to whistle. "I can't do anything about it. It won't boil any quicker." Her voice was unsteady but she was nowhere near to tears. "Does he shout at everyone like that? How do you manage to work with him?"

Faulkner pretended to look for some papers. "Never call him 'Likely' and he's not so keen on chief. He likes this new brand of coffee and, most of all, he likes to talk. So we give him this coffee and encourage him to smoke his pipe. Never ignore his reminiscences. They've got more police savvy than you'll find in a dozen copies of Moriarty. And, by the way, he's the only good governor I've worked for and, although we joke about it, he is one of our best detectives. Unfortunately, the governor can't do people. He can't get along with them at all. That's our job really, to deal with all the bits he throws off the cart. I spend most of my time explaining to people that he didn't really say what they thought he said."

"His wife's supposed to be very good with him. Is it true that when things are difficult, you telephone her and suggest that the chief would like something on the side with his dinner?"

Faulkner felt the colour come to his face. "Good God, girl. I don't know where you heard such a thing as that." He wasn't sure that she understood the rumour. "Come on, you'll need a pencil and notepad and you can bring the biscuits. And don't speak unless he speaks to you." He gave her his best smile. "Ding-ding. Round Two."

Storey was standing at the window with his jacket tails pushed back and his hands in his trouser pockets. He said, without turning around, "I've built up the fire. It should get going before long. You might as well tell us. Who's your uncle?"

She cleared her throat. "A rather fat lady brought up some raspberry flan with cream. She said it was for you."

He grunted. "Did she tell you that I am one the first detectives, outside a metropolitan area, to be given the rank detective inspector? Normally, it's just inspector and everyone knows they're a detective."

"No, she didn't say that."

"Strange. I've told her many times. Who is your uncle?"

"My name is actually Dorothy Hilary Holden but most people call me D.H."

"Holden?" He turned around, his mouth slightly open with surprise. "You are the niece," he began incredulously, "of the Commissioner of the London's Metropolitan Police?"

"That was," she began, pausing to swallow deeply, "a little bit of a white lie." She winced, trying to win him over. "Just a teeny one."

He put his head to one side. "Is the truth better or worse?"

"It's probably a whole lot worse, chief."

He sat down, put his elbows on his blotter and buried his face in his hands. He felt the dust, shaken from his books, settle on the back of his neck. When he emerged, he said softly, "Good grief. They have put the Met Commissioner's daughter in my office."

Nobody spoke. Police work carried on throughout the rest of the building. Outside, traffic bunched at the railway station crossroads, folk complained on buses and the newsboys on street corners were selling papers about Eden's resignation from the cabinet. The clock on the mantelpiece ticked the seconds by but, although everyone wanted her chime to break the silence, she refused to allow it.

"It sounds much worse than it is," Miss Holden tried. She had lost count of the times she had worked through this reaction. "I'm not his favourite or anything like that." She glanced at Faulkner for support but he was looking down at his lap as he filled his pipe. His face was lined and serious. Like his governor, he was finding it difficult to make sense of the conspiracy. She pressed on. "He told the last lot that took me on that he'd be happy if he never saw me again. But they still sent me back. That was a newspaper. It's not as if you can spoil me or make me any worse than I am." She waited for Faulkner to look up but he didn't. "OK if I pour the tea and hand round the biscuits now? Chief, don't forget your dessert."

He knew that Janine wouldn't put up with him making things difficult for the girl. He guessed that the two would be in cahoots before the end of the week, trading news over the telephone and asking him to carry packages he knew nothing about. He sensed that Faulkner's silence indicated that he was already on the young woman's side.

Storey tried to show no change in his expression. "She can't smoke in here, sergeant. It would be indelicate."

"Couldn't agree more, governor," Faulkner replied with a wink to the girl.

"And she's got the better chair. Did you see that?"

"This time only, gov. We'll make something of her, you'll see."

Storey's pipe was going well. "Yes. With her connections, she's bound to go far so, yes, it's our job to make something of her." He pushed the tart her way. "Here, eat this. They've probably laced it with something gone off."

Chapter Four

Storey leaned back in his office chair and looked down to consider the strain on his waistcoat buttons. "Edith Winterton, alias Snowflake, lived at 239 Denning Flats. It's her correct address. Her mother and father are dead but she had a boyfriend, Bob. Faulkner, I'll give you the names of two friends, letter writers, and you can record them on file. Every Monday she visited the Red Rose restaurant on Eastern Parade. Two or three weeks ago, a woman who may or may not have been Snowflake walked into the Red Rose with a photo of me and asked the proprietor to identify it. He couldn't. Two days later she came in and said that I was a chief inspector at central police station but she didn't know my name." He looked up and, looking to the girl, said, "I put them right about the chief." He asked, "Interesting?"

"Very," Faulkner agreed. "Why did she think the proprietor would recognise your photo?"

Storey made a face. "That's our work done for today." He stood up. "Lady, you will telephone the Head Constable at his home and brief him accordingly, with my respects. The call will give him an opportunity to chat about how you are settling in. I'm sure he'll want you to do that. You may offer a true and detailed account but you will not tell him that you are forbidden to set foot in this police station tomorrow or that you will spend all day at the Red Rose restaurant, observing and listening. You understand why you must keep this from him?"

"Of course, chief. If we're to catch this murderer before the county police, we've got to keep one jump ahead."

"Very good," said Faulkner.

Storey agreed. "Very good. But you are not a police officer and certainly not a detective. You are not experienced enough to ask questions at the Red Rose without revealing our hand. So: you will not ask questions. If you ask one question, I will threaten to throw you off the team. I'm sure that's understood."

"Threaten?"

Faulkner assured her, "Of course, the governor never goes as far as actually throwing anyone off the team once they're aboard. Good Lord, we put up with Harry for two years."

"Miss Holden, do you feel you know enough about this case?" Storey asked. He was bringing his coat over his shoulders and looking around for his hat. He felt in his pockets for his gloves.
. "I am sure you don't. You may familiarise yourself with Sergeant Faulkner's file before you go home. Don't forget to lock up."

Mrs Storey had chosen a dress that, when she moved in the right way, would convince her husband she was wearing no knickers. She didn't expect him home for forty minutes and she practised the sways and bobs as she toured the rooms of their flat. She knew that he liked her to reveal a corset when he watched her undress, so she had spent last month's pocket money with her little old lady in Arthur Street. The dear had run up a pretty example which laced up the front and made much more of Janine's breasts than Janine deserved. She checked in every mirror she passed and it was so.

When Storey came in, he looked quiet, weary and down in the dumps. She took his coat, brought some fresh tobacco from the cupboard, then sat him at the kitchen table while she fussed with some last touches to their lamp chops.

"I've been looking round the Denning Flats this afternoon."

"I know. I rang Faulkner and he told me." Janine was straining the veg over the sink. She leaned against the rim, trying to make just a little more of her rear than was natural.

"They're so cramped, no room to breathe. You couldn't row without half a dozen neighbours hearing."

"We're very lucky."

"Do you mind living in a flat?" He was speaking with his unlit pipe in his mouth. "Does it get on your nerves? We could find a house, do it up, move in."

"We've seen so many couples do that, my love, and what have they all done? Filled every room with children.. That's not us. And don't pretend you're not happy here because I know you are."

Storey accepted his dinner, picked up his knife and fork and let her take the pipe from his teeth. "No, no. I wasn't suggesting anything. Just checking, I suppose. This looks good." He added, good naturedly, "Everything looks good from where I am sitting," and, because she was so practised, Janine managed to blush.

"Why aren't you more angry?" she asked.

Storey spoke while he ate. "I was to begin with but anger can only go so far when you're challenged. I took on Haynes eighteen months ago when people noticed he was having trouble with reading. He puts in things that aren't there. Sometimes, he just gets the words the wrong way round and doesn't realise it. He's still a good policeman but he's best when someone's with him and he needs to be given time. Now, he's back in uniform but I expect him back before Christmas. Then we'll have to repeat all the work that we've done with him. Or, rather, Faulkner will. I like this mustard. Is it new?"

"You're not supposed to have mustard with lamb so I asked Mulberry's to make me up something mild."

He was chewing. "Hmm. It's very good."

"Love, why don't you stop, just for a second, and wash it down with your coffee?"

"You're not supposed to have coffee until afterwards," he joked. "They've found a good blend of coffee in the office. You must get Faulkner to tell you about it."

He was only half way through his dinner but he put the knife and fork down, sat back and patted his belly. "You'll make me fat, Mrs Storey."

"How will Paul St John manage?"

"He won't. And it's harsh to expect him to. If he's not back within a fortnight, I shall set out the circumstances very clearly to our Head Constable, and demand his return. I shall go to the Chairman of the Watch if necessary. His Sir -Knight-ship owes me a favour."

Storey resumed his dinner. "I see three loose ends in this case. Faulkner says two and one untidy knot, which is probably a better analysis. You see, two questions will keep coming back to us and the thing won't be solved until we can nail them with answers."

Janine brought her knife and fork together on her empty plate."Why did Edith Snowflake go to Coldwater Place to begin with?"

"Exactly. Faulkner saw that as a key point from the start. And then, why did she, or someone else, take my photo into the Red Rose?"

"And Faulkner's untidy knot?"

Storey shrugged. "She came to see me. Was that part of the plan or the spanner in the works?"

When the telephone interrupted their dessert, Janine answered it and called through from their little hallway. "It's half past nine and Miss Holden asks if she can go home."

Storey pulled one of his faces. Janine replied for him, "Yes, of course you can, dear. The detective inspector is grateful that you stayed so. late."

"I didn't know," he protested before she had time to put the question.

"I can't believe you gave her a detention."

"I didn't. I said she could read through Faulkner's paperwork. I had no idea she'd stay this late. Come on, we'll go through to the fire with our brandy and cheeses."

The logs were blazing and they pulled up two armchairs to make a cosy enclave. They checked - brandies, the cheeses, fresh tobacco and a good supply of matches - as if they were looking forward to a long voyage. Storey sat in the master chair while Janine settled herself at his feet, knowing that, before long, his hand would fall and check for the ribbing of her corset.

"Were you serious?" she asked. "They wouldn't give you permission to live out, would they?"

"They've been more obliging recently for officers approaching retirement. It would help if we were in a family police house. They'd see an advantage in moving us out then. And, if I'm going to ask, I need to ask before the borough is taken over."

"Is that likely?"

"Not in the next year or two, no. But I'm sure I'll see it before my time is up. There'll be another war, pet. We know that, don't we? That's what Eden's resignation is all about. He knows we're getting it wrong. We're heading straight for it and that's why he's gone. This year or next, the year after maybe? The police forces of England will be brought together - in the national interest, they'll say. Of course, if we lose the war, it won't matter because the fascists will run everything anyhow. And if we win? The government will forget to return things to how they were. Britain will have one giant national police force and Inspector Storey will be seen crying in his beer."

"Brian, that's all horrible to think about," she said unsteadily but seconds later, knocked a knuckle against his knee and decided, "You must ask to move out at once."

"Whose turn is it to read?" he asked.

"Yours, unless you're too tired."

"No, no. We must keep to the schedule. Do you fancy a few pages from *Bleak House*? Really, your Thomas Hardy's too grim for this evening. Do you mind, really?"

He was happy to avoid the nine o'clock news. The nation at large was too concerned about Anthony Eden's withdrawal from Chamberlain's government and, while the wireless would certainly make less of it than the newspapers, it wasn't a controversy that he wanted in his sitting-room. At eleven, he would turn it on for dance music from one of the big hotels in London. They were broadcasting from the Grosvenor tonight, he thought.

He paused in the middle of Dickens and closed his eyes. Janine wondered if he had fallen asleep. When his eyes came to, she said, "Your girl was expelled from St Mary's."

"A convent?"

"No, dear. Wantage. It's the country's most exclusive school for young ladies. It even has its own railway trains for the girls at the beginnings and ends of terms. Daughters of kings and queens go there."

"She doesn't talk like it. She's got a hint of American slap-dash in her voice. What terrible things did she do?"

"She used an American gadget."

"An American gadget? What on earth does that mean? No one can be expelled from school because they've used a gadget."

"I think it was the American bit that counted against her. Mrs Cairncross in the Boots Booklovers Library says she probably behaved in an unladylike way."

Storey grunted. "Conduct unbecoming."

"Mrs Cairncross telephoned hither and thither but couldn't find the details."

"Yes, they have a tremendous network," he conceded. "We could telephone hither and thither and never speak to the right person. Janine, how do I handle her? I've no experience with girls. You've just said it -I can't be doing with being a father. I haven't the foggiest."

"You give her back her confidence. Then, you'll see. She'll do the rest."

Bedtime came before ten o'clock. There would be no Grosvenor Hotel, after all. They left the bedroom door open so that the warmth of the sitting-room fire might take off the chill, and they made do with one bedside lamp. Janine's hours of gentle, patient teasing had done its work and when the couple slept they found the comfy lumps and cushions of limb and flesh which, through ten years of marriage, each had identified as favourite places. The noise of street traffic was never far away - their bedroom was at the front (a nuisance) and only two floors above a busy pavement - but if they disturbed after midnight, they expected the reassuring sounds of distant railways and tugs working the river.

At half past one, the telephone was ringing in the hall. Storey's feet were on the floor before he was awake. He found his slippers without looking and was rubbing his eyes open as he padded over the carpet. Funny how a telephone bell can sound sad or urgent, panicky even, depending on the mood of the caller.

"Mr Storey, I've been silly. You better come quick."

"Where are you, Miss Holden?"

"In the call box along from the Red Rose. There's something going on in there and I think they've seen me. Mr Storey, I wouldn't ring you unless ..."

Chapter Five

"I know that. I want you to stay at the telephone box. I will send a police car to collect you. Sergeant Faulkner and I won't be far behind and we'll take a look around."

He dialled all the twos and gave instructions for a car to be dispatched.

Janine was already in the kitchen. "You're waiting for a flask of hot coffee, Brian. It's not two o'clock and you're not going without it." They had known each other for more than thirty years, yet she still spoke his name as if she wanted to end it with 'd'.

Storey dialled Faulkner's number, got it wrong, cursed and dialled again.

Faulkner had a pool car for the evening. He collected Storey en route and, at seven minutes past two, drew up behind the black patrol car, fifty yards from the late night restaurant. The light still burned in the telephone box.

Before he had climbed out of the car, Storey had worked out that the girl was missing.

An officer approached from the patrol car. He looked warm, dry and well able to manage his comfort throughout a nightshift. "No sign of the lass, as simple as that, gov. She weren't here at all when I got here. I took a scoot round. You know, looking for shoes or a handbag, but there's nothing. Not even a hanky. Now, the Willow Street nick are saying I've got to wait for a bloodhound. That seems a bit of a fuss, gov, don't it? Important is she, this lass?"

"Well, now, that depends, constable. If she were your daughter, I guess she'd be important. Tell me, did you see any activity around the back of the restaurant? While you were 'scooting round' for the missing lady, I mean."

"The back of the restaurant, sir?"

"Yes, I know. It is complicated. Why are you wearing your cap?"

"I've been driving, gov."

"You drive, you wear your cap. You get out, you put your helmet on. Another difficult notion, I know. What time were you expecting refs?"

"Two o'clock, sir." He'd heard that Storey could be difficult.

"Well, you wait here and the sergeant and I will arrange some sandwiches from the restaurant. Sergeant Faulkner, this way."

As they marched across the road to the Red Rose, Storey commented, "To make matters clear, sergeant, your detective inspector has managed to lose the Met Commissioner's daughter. You might call it the one moment in his lifetime that calls for straightforward action. Did I ever tell you about the time I worked with the Navy Shore Patrols? No? Oh, it was such an education."

He pushed through the restaurant door. While Faulkner cleared the last customers and put up the closed sign, Storey marched straight to the kitchen.

"Attention!" he bawled. "No more messing about, Bert Williams, no more shillying around. I know you and you know me. Back in '21 you were arrested for a gambling fraud."

Williams had been sleeping on crossed arms at the work table and didn't understand what was happening. He pushed his chair backwards as he got to his feet. "What is this? Who says you..." He put his hands up and started to walk backwards.

"The detectives questioned you for six hours in the city central police station, then asked me to sit in with you. They thought that a couple of hour's chitti-chat might loosen your tongue. I was the greenhorn, you see. They wanted to see what

I'd get out of you, I suppose. We understand each other, you and I. I've always said that if we ever met again, we'll get on fine. Now, I'm in a right mess and I think you know the answers. No please, I haven't time for you to think about it." The man had backed himself to a wall. Storey got in close and delivered a sharp, knuckled crack to his nose.

Williams went down without a sound. When Storey hauled him up and propped him against the wall, the man had his hands over his face and blood was running down his chin and wrists. "Take your hands away," Storey demanded. He pushed them aside with one hand and, with the other, shot a second punch on top of the first. This time, Williams howled like a kicked dog and started to crawl away.

"Sit on that chair and do as you're told!" Storey shouted. "I know you can take any amount of this, so I'm going to start on your kitchen. This is going to be really painful so let's make it fun. Every time I smash something, I want you to shout how much it's costing you."

Williams held up his hands. "No, no. No look. You're an honest policeman, I know that, Mr Storey. All this, it has been a dreadful mistake. It's a misunderstanding between us. I should have made it plain that I want to help you as much as I can. I don't know much but I'll talk for God's Sake. For God's Sake, Mr Storey, you've got to give a man the chance to talk."

Storey came close again and smiled. "Sergeant," he called politely.

Faulkner stepped into the kitchen. "Crying out loud, governor."

"Yes it is a mess. That is the only drawback to the Navy method. Please detail our constable outside to put this man in the cells. I'll be ready to speak with him in the morning."

Faulkner clutched the shoulder of the man's overall. "On your feet, sunshine."

"Keeping a disorderly house, I've good reason to suspect."

"Governor!" squawked the prisoner. "I'm not a pimp. For God Sake, Mr Storey.

"But you don't understand, Williams. In less than forty minutes, I shall be called to my Head Constable's office and in there, I'll find the Commissioner of London's Metropolitan Police. He'll want to know what steps I've taken to find his daughter. I need a prisoner, Williams, don't I?"

"Mr Storey, she's not been kidnapped. She heard two of my customers talking and she decided to follow them."

"Follow them?"

"D.I. Skelton and one of his constables had arranged to meet someone in here."

"Did they recognise Miss Holden?"

"Why would they? They noticed her, certainly. Who wouldn't; she looked so good in her costume."

"Costume?"

"I've taken her on was a waitress, Mr Storey. Look, my Julie ran out on me this evening. Three minutes later, your girl came in and asked for the job. Is that wrong? But I'm sure the visitor recognised her. He came in the back way, took one look at her and left a message with me for the detectives. He'd changed his mind. He wouldn't meet them in here. Suddenly. I'm alone in my restaurant. Skelton and his sidekick have run out of the place and Miss Holden has whipped of her pinny and cap and says that she's not allowed out after two."

"How did she manage to follow them? She's no car."

"I've been storing an old motorcycle at the back. I mean, she was welcome to it, Mr Storey. I've no complaint. You know, I was surprised she got it going."

"What were your customers talking about?"

"How would I know, gov?"

"Williams, you know everything. The murder of one woman and the disappearance of another point to this place being a den of ungodliness. But we'll have time to discuss these matters at length. Right now, where do I need to go? Where will I find Miss Holden?"

"This thing, Mr Storey, I think it's bigger than you think."

"So tell me where to go."

He took a breath. "Shorthouse Quay, Mr Storey, but I want you to be careful."

"Let him go, sergeant. Williams, we have a constable outside who has given up his refreshment stop. You owe him his supper, Williams. I want you to stuff him until he goes purple. He's a greedy pig but I'm sure you'll be able to fill him up."

"Of course, Mr Storey, I shall see him the right. I want you all to know that policemen are forever welcome in the Red Rose restaurant. Please, tell your friends."

The Bantam Popular crawled to the top of the black bank where Faulkner brought it to a stop with the handbrake. "We're in a car from the borough's pool, gov, and Shorthouse is a city beat, not even county."

Storey agreed with the sentiment. "I've got previous for trespass," he conceded.

"Gov, sit here and drink Janine's coffee. Let me take a look around."

"You think I'll get us into trouble?"

"Governor, you have worked with the greatest detectives in England, but someone on this team has got to apply the brakes."

Storey felt a little like a truculent child. "I want to know what connects 239 Denning Flats, 18 Coldwater Place and the Red Rose cafe. I want to know why Edith Winterton came to me in the first place and I want to know why I am sitting in the dark on a slag heap overlooking Shorthouse Quay."

His sergeant opened the car door. "I'll see what I can find out."

Storey pulled at his upturned collar, regathered Grandma Depaillier's scarf around his neck and pressed his hands in the coat pocket for some seconds before deciding to pack his pipe from a new sheath of tobacco. He expected Faulkner to be a good twenty minutes. In spite of his sergeant's explicit instruction not to play with the heater, which Storey had no hope of understanding, he fiddled with the knobs until the rumble of warm air satisfied him that right things were happening.

He heard Faulkner curse as loose coke gave way underfoot and he had to throw out an arm or land on his back. The old hand would go no further until his hat was put right on his head and the debris shaken from his trousers. Then Faulkner's grey figure disappeared into the shadows.

Chickens? Storey could hear chickens. What were chickens doing on a quayside? Chickens couldn't abide water. He tried to get out but realised that it would have been too much of a clamber. "I'm sure I can hear chickens," he muttered and pulled his scarf closer to his chin.

The creaks and stretches of wet ropes were like some hideous section of the orchestra attempting to tune up. An unkempt cat patrolled the quayside. She knew, for food and warmth, she'd be better off on the unlit freighter but every option for jumping aboard seemed more risky than she thought sensible. There was no sign of anyone else on the quay.

"All sorts could come ashore and we'd be none the wiser," he muttered through his teeth. He struck a match and within a few seconds the inside of the little car was blue with tobacco smoke.

Faulkner walked, almost casually, between the old storehouses and workshops with no attempt to conceal himself. If he had been in another place, at another time, he might have been out for a stroll. He showed an interest in the abandoned safe, half sunken in the mud behind a brick-built coal bunker. He took out a hanky and cleaned the brass plate until he was able to read the manufacturer and the date. (It was the sort of thing that would interest Sergeant Horndean at Willow Place.) He found the old motorcycle, still warm, propped against a chain link fence and followed her footsteps in the black mud.

"Do you recognise them?"

"Good grief, Miss Holden, what are doing in there?"

"Watching those three men in the back of the bunker. Do you know them?"

"The tall one is Doug Skelton, head of the county's detective branch and his constable is Abel Sharp. He's boxed against the Imperial Services. He should be a sergeant, by rights. Is it safe in there? Come on out."

"As long as I don't lean too far forward."

"Come on out," he said again.

"I think it's out of kilter but I shan't fall. Those men are buying information from the third man. He came to the cafe, saw me and ran away."

"Come on, Miss. There's nothing suspicious here but it's private business. Skelton won't thank us for scaring away his squealer."

"I've got his car number. ELN 34"

"Well done. It's time to go home."

"The chief's going to be cross about this," she said, sure she was in trouble. "I shouldn't have telephoned him."

"He'd rather you didn't say chief."

At a quarter to five, the pool car drew up at St Anne's Court and the occupants disappeared into the foyer. When Janine heard them on the staircase, she tipped a saucer of bacon over the pan of frying kidneys and turned up the sauce.

"I've wasted your time, I'm sorry," the girl was saying as they walked through the door.

Storey said, "Oh, something far worse. You allowed your enthusiasm to get the better of you. I shall mention this for the first and last time. Enthusiasm is no excuse."

"I know that, chief."

"But you redeemed yourself by asking for help when you needed it. Sergeant Faulkner and I are impressed, truly. Sit down everyone. I'll take your coats. Miss Holden, my wife would like to take you shopping for the day. This will be a chance to reflect before you work further with us."

Janine turned and delivered four plates to the cramped breakfast table. "It's lovely to meet you, Debbie." One look at their expressions told her that she was the first to use her Christian name.

"Most people say D.H."

"Well, I won't be calling you that. Deborah if we are among strangers but otherwise Debbie. Now, I don't want to hear it from the boys. I want to hear the story as you tell it." She looked up from her plate. "I've forgotten the dry toast."

"The inspector can be trusted with dry toast," said Storey pushing himself back from the table. "Carry on, Deborah."

Janine retrieved the conversation. "Yes, you spoke to me on the telephone at half past eight."

"Then I walked through the city centre to the Red Rose."

"On your own?" Faulkner put in. "It's more than a mile and a half through some of the seediest streets and it must have been close to ten before you got there."

"I knew that I would need a good excuse to sit in the cafe all day tomorrow, so I asked the chef for a job. I didn't like him, Mr Storey, not at all. He put me in a black dress with a pinny and a white hat and told me to start straight away. At first, I thought I had been really lucky because, in less than an hour, two suspicious characters took a corner table. I didn't realise that they were policemen at the start but it soon became obvious. They had arranged to meet a stranger who was going to give them information."

Faulkner grunted. "How do you know that? Tell us just what they said."

Deborah cleared her throat and quoted, "We're not going to give him the money until we're sure he knows."

"We've all done it, gov?"

Storey returned to the table with cut triangles of unbuttered toast. "It sounds as if they knew what he had to offer. That's interesting. I remember, once Evanshaw paid for information and immediately got the money back. It's an amusing tale."

Janine held a hand over his. "But a tale for another day, darling. We're listening to Debbie's adventure."

"I spoilt things because the visitor came in the back of the Red Rose and recognised me at once."

"That can only be from the police station," Faulkner said. "Did you recognise him?"

"Not at all. Minutes later, we were all racing towards the docks. The county detectives in their car, the visitor following and me on that crock of a motorcycle, miles behind."

"You got his car number. That was good," Storey said. "What happened at Shorthouse Quay?"

"I was too late. I couldn't find my way around and I'd only just spotted them when Mr Faulkner joined me."

Faulkner commented, "I am sure they passed over the money."

"Which means they've received the information. It's Skelton's investigation and there's nothing wrong in what he did." Storey had finished his breakfast. He leant back and patted the belly of his waistcoat. "But we have another loose end, ladies and gentlemen. Why was their informant so worried when he spotted Deborah?"

Chapter Six

They should sell this place and turn it into a bank, thought Storey as he climbed the back stairs to the top floor. It would make a good bank with strong-rooms in the dungeons and a readymade muniments room for customers' files, not to mention a sumptuous select for board meetings. Yes, and it had a good position on a busy corner overlooking the town square. Then he heard the canteen cook empty a dustbin of old food down the waste chute. "They'd even find a use for that, I'm sure."

When Storey emerged onto the fifth landing, the ever so silent door of the select opened an inch or two and, using a carefully placed mirror, the attendant member of the Watch Committee observed his progress along the expensive carpet and past the portraits of previous Heads and Chairs and gentlemen surgeons. Likely was tempted to dash along the corridor and expose the nosy parker in the act. But the Head Constable's lady clerk had already opened her door and was drawing him in.

"Oh, I did laugh! When you shouted, 'Don't tell me that woman under the cats is my Boy Scout!' I thought it was one of your best outbursts, Mr Storey."

Storey hooked his gloves and overcoat on the hat stand and checked his wristwatch. "I'm sure I said hats. I would never have mentioned cats, not in that way."

The woman stood at her desk and tried to persuade a bundle of papers at all angles to form a perfect sheaf by banging their feet on the desktop.

"She's driving me nuts, Miranda," he said. "She calls me chief, all the time. It makes me feel like a New York squad boss who sends his men out on snowy nights."

The inner door of the suite opened, revealing the Head Constable with a cigar. "Come in, Likely. Last night's docket make interesting reading. You were up to something?"

"Nothing that produced results, sir. I may have trodden on county's toes so it's probably better that I don't tell you."

He waved Storey to an armchair as he walked around to sit behind his expansive desk. The Head preferred paraffin heaters to open fires; Storey was sure that explained the perpetual cigars. "I'm sure you'd be more comfortable with your pipe. Please don't hesitate. Now, I want you to call me Roger."

"Yes, Roger." He made a large lap and set out his pipe, tobacco pouch of Moroccan leather, Captain Webb matches and his solid silver tamper. Smoking in an office as plush as this one wasn't a delight to be hurried. He wondered if a Head Constable merited a lavatory of his own; then realised that chivalry would demand that it should be passed on to benefit his lady clerk.

"We've cress sandwiches coming up," the Head was saying, "with that special mustard that Mulberry's make up for your wife. Pamela heard about it and ordered some. Really, very nice. Really, you and Janine must come round one evening. Don't you think this direct reporting to me, rather than through the station, is working well? I like it, Likely. I like the feel of it."

"I can see that, sir. Yes, very much the feel."

"Likely, I know I have depleted your reserves. Man, I've had to. But it gives you more elbow room. You must concede that you and Faulkner have more room to move."

"And no less work."

Now, he became an excited boy, thrilled by the prospect of a new game. His clenched fists went up and down as if they were driving pistons. "Which is why I have said Likely must have any resources from across this borough. I've already sent the order out. Whatever Likely needs, we must give him. Men, bicycles, typewriters, first choice of the tables in the canteen."

"Has this anything to do with my supervision of the Metropolitan Commissioner's daughter?"

"The truth is, we all -and I am speaking for the entire borough force here, if not for the borough forces of England - we need you to solve this murder on your own. Not so much behind the county's back. More, under their nose. Now, I want to make it clear that we have the full backing of the Watch Committee. Sir Jason is a stalwart, Likely, a true stalwart. But all minor police forces are under threat. Damn it, we've no room to be clever. That's the trouble. And governments these days like people to do clever things. Aeroplane tracking systems. Television. Colour shows at the pictures. Ministers love it, Likely."

He sighed and leaned forward, elbows on his unused blotter, shoes resting delicately on the mahogany foot rest beneath the desk. "I am telling you this because moves are afoot. Danvers-Wright on the hill has been having lunches. He's taken people fishing. He's had conferences in corners and found excuses to keep me out. Last week, I was called to Scotland Yard to observe their new nerve centre - it's a bank of telephones, Likely, with a map on the wall and a wireless no one can understand - and I was cornered by a bandit in round spectacles and pig-gloves. Home office accountant, he turned out to be, but he didn't say that. He wanted me to understand that it would make no difference. I would be a superintendent reporting to Danvers-Wright instead of a Watch Committee. Apart from that, day-to-day business would carry on much the same. Do you know what he said, this four-eyed twit? He said no-one wants to talk of Head Constables these days. What do you make of that? Likely, I'm a turkey being fattened for Christmas. We need you to show that murders are best solved by small teams following the obvious, most straightforward route. Nothing fancy. No little cards with orange dots on the corners or maps with coloured pins joined up by bits of wool brought in from home when the super's wife has done with them. I am not making too much of it, Likely, when I say that we are defending the heritage of our land here. You, Likely. You are defending everything learned throughout England's proud history of policing. Damn it, Storey, I've been a Head Constable for ten years. Do I want to end up as a superintendent? Why should they do it to me?"

Storey watched an idea creep into his head. His ears twitched to one side as he weighed it and, finding it to be a not unpleasant thought, he smiled. "Would you like to be a chief inspector, Likely? I could apply to the Watch Committee for funding and designation. I can't promise. Not even Head Constables can promise it but would you like it?"

Storey thought, you've no chance of that and you know it. "I would rather catch this killer, sir."

"Oh, well fielded, Likely, and a good answer!"

Spring snapped in with a bite that year. Something more than an innocent nippiness hurried heavily clothed mothers and infants along the town pavements, sent gossips into shop doorways rather than corner pavements and kept the men at their desks and workbenches. Young noses had March colds and young sleeves bulged with bunched up hankies. Everyone said that everything was going to get worse.

The world news was so bad -so almightily bad- that anything positive, like a victory for the local team or the announcement that a hitherto anonymous housewife from a street that everyone passed by had won a cookery competition in a national magazine, was celebrated out of all proportion to its legacy.

This morning everyone was talking about four girls sacked from Woolworths but, because no one could get at the truth, unpalatable rumours of betrayal, thieving and buns in some ovens spread, almost visibly, up and down the pavements at a brisk walking pace. Standing on the police station steps, overlooking the sloping courtyard and, beyond, the High Street,

Storey was told off by a woman at the back of the baker's van for listening to stories against innocent young women. He allowed himself a smug look; Janine would learn the truth and Storey would know before suppertime.

He decided to take twenty minutes with his pipe instead of a lunch. He walked down the steps and installed himself at the end of a wooden bench. A grass bank behind him provided some shelter from the cold but he still spruced up his scarf and collar and made sure coat buttons were done up. These days, he reflected, he so rarely had the chance to enjoy a good pipe.

As he sat and watched, on the edge of a daydream, a humble Austin motorcar, round shaped and in need of a clean, climbed the driveway and naively declared herself to be ELN 34. Here was Skelton's informant.

"Dominic Worth," said Sergeant Miller, taking a seat at the end of a long walk with a dog from the pound. "You wouldn't think a man like that would have fingers in so many pies, would you, inspector? He looks - what'd you say? - humble? Yet, he's on your tribunal and our Watch Committee and he's part of the team looking into county's money bags. Yes, Mr Dominic Worth, short, stubby, podgy-faced and red-chubby-cheeked. With a head so round that his spectacles keep slipping off. There's something of a poem in him, don't you think?"

Storey realised that the sergeant enjoyed pushing his luck, bending familiarity to the verge of impertinence but always keeping safe from the line that might draw criticism. Neither man liked much that was in the other.

"Sergeant Miller, I think you should be a snout for the county police. You've a way with words."

The two men watched the porky figure progress from the parking bay to the concrete steps of the police station.

"You see, inspector, I can't get it out of my head that Worth, not me, is a spy."

Storey coughed and prepared to return indoors. "You're quite right, sergeant. Do you know, he peeped over my shoulder

60

when I was drawing a naked woman in the middle of our last meeting? I wouldn't be surprised if he has already told the Italians."

Miller laughed and tugged at his mongrel on a string.

Storey walked indoors and enquired at the desk, "Mr Worth?"

"Lavs," croaked the constable without lifting his face from a ledger. Then he felt Storey's presence, straightened his back and replied, "He went to the lavatories, inspector, although I may have missed him going up in the lift. Mr Worth always works on the fifth floor."

"Thank you, constable."

Storey stepped into the lift and when the doors were closing Worth squeezed in, uncomfortable and short of breath. "Thank goodness we're alone, Storey. I must warn you. The detectives looking into the murder of Edith Winterton would like you to be a casualty of the investigation. I can't keep it to myself. I've got to warn people. It's come from the top."

Storey responded politely. "Thank you. Forewarned is forearmed, they say." The doors opened and Storey stepped across the threshold.

Worth grabbed his sleeve. "No, no. It's far bigger than you think. Come and see me. I must have half an hour across the desk with Miranda. Then, come and see me, Storey."

"Of course, I will. In three quarters of an hour, do you think?"

Sergeant Faulkner had his head down, updating his office journal from the scribbled notes in his pocket book. "Afternoon, gov," he said without looking up. "I'll be with you right away."

Storey stood in the middle of the room. His coat was open, his hat was off and he looked cheerfully untidy. "Where is she?"

"You said that she had to shop with Mrs Storey."

He slapped his hat against his thigh. "Yes, damn it. I need her. I've got a job for her."

Faulkner closed the journal and got to his feet. "Can I help?"

"No, no, it's a job for her, Faulkner. Do you think she'll phone in?"

"Mrs Storey might when they get back from the shops. Often, she does. She likes to know what you're up to, governor."

"If she does, I've a message for the girl. Now, come into the office and leave the coffee. We've no time for that."

He disappeared into his room, hung up his hat and coat, taking his gloves from his pocket and giving them a peg of their own. Then he put his head outside the door. "What am I saying? Nothing's urgent. Bring the coffee. We need to spend some time thinking."

King George VI looked down from the calendar, Dixie Dean was curling at the edges because his photograph hadn't been framed and Storey's medal for boules, usually polished without fail, hadn't seen a duster this year. Storey was lying back in his chair; when he moved his head, Faulkner lost him behind the piles of books on his desk.

Storey waited until his pipe was well on the go, then took it from his mouth and said, "Your man at the quayside is my man on the Poynton Committee. He's just collared me in the lift and warned me that county is after my head."

"Nothing new in that, gov, but it won't be you they're after; they'll want H.C." Faulkner was sitting forward with his knees wide apart so that he could fill his pipe between his legs.

"I know. You're right and the Head's got the same nerves. I spent this morning with him. Come on, Faulkner. Worth warns me against county but last night he was taking money off them. Come on, man, work it out."

Two telephones in the outside office rang at the same time as Storey's. The two detectives could hear the corridors filling with people. Someone was shouting 'No!' on the stairs.

Storey barked down the phone. "Detective inspector!"

He listened, slammed the telephone down and dialled again.

"Lock down, Sergeant Miller!"

The desk sergeant was brisk and attentive. "Already in place, inspector. I have the names of everyone who's left the station in the last twenty minutes."

"Good man. Don't be distracted. Stay at that desk." He looked at the King and shook his head. "On your feet, Faulkner. Dominic Worth is dead in the Watch Committee's select."

When, in the nineteen-twenties Tristan Evanshaw said that there were good bodies and bad ones and Superintendent Ben Graythorpe, who did his best detecting from 28-31, described them as either clean or dirty, they weren't marking their ability to turn a man's stomach. Each murder does that; let no one tell you otherwise. Those two experienced hands were taking a colder look at the corpse and asking it to give up the clues to its death. A clean body tells you it's a stabbing but a dirty body, Superintendent Graythorpe explained to cohort after cohort of students, requires the detective to take on the skills of an archaeologist before he can be sure of the time of death, the length of the blade or the light in the dead man's eyes.

The remains of sixty year old Dominic Worth looked clean at the start but ended up dirty. In the silent, expensively furnished select, where members of the Watch Committee, and nobody else, came to do business, waste time, agree alliances and bury old wounds, Detective Inspector Storey knelt over the body and peered closely at the knife wound to the man's chest.

The Head Constable came in close from the crowd and whispered, "They won't let me give you the case, Likely. The Watch Committee will insist that I bring someone in."

The reply was as even as it was determined. "The Watch Committee can do what it likes. This man asked to meet me in this room. I should have been here, listening to him. Instead, I am here and he is dead. I'm going to find who slaughtered him. Your Watch Committee would be foolish to borrow a detective from county or elsewhere, but since I cannot stop them, I'd better have the thing solved before the new man gets here." He rested back on his ankles. "I don't think I'm far from doing that," he said. "Could everyone leave the room, please? Except for you, Head. And if Sergeant Faulkner could have a look round. Background, sergeant. Look for the background."

"Already on the job, inspector."

"What do you think, Head? Worth dropped like a stone, I'd say. Unusual in a stabbing. Yes, here we are, he fell back against the wallpaper, see? So the attacker was standing in front of him. Talking? Arguing? A dispute that could not be solved so out comes the knife? What Graythorpe would call a good clean corpse but, I say, a little gory for the fifth floor, don't you think, Head?"

"I - I put you in charge of the case, detective inspector. And damn what the Watch Committee says." He sounded like a school prefect making the first brave decision of his life.

Chapter Seven

Storey was in his pyjamas and nearly asleep. The music on the National Programme was fading in and out, as if he were listening from the hotel kitchen and the waiters' doors kept swinging open and closed. Janine, who had been in her dressing gown all evening, was seated between his legs and working miracles with socks that looked beyond repair.

He opened half an eye. "We can afford new ones."

"We can afford new ones because I darn old ones." She reminded him, "Your mother didn't live through the war in Belgium," then wished she hadn't. "Bowly's good."

His eye returned to its closed position. "He croons," he said. "Sergeant Miller was telling his cronies this afternoon. Al Bowly is a good crooner."

He stretched a slippered foot towards the fireplace. "What did you find out?"

"It was a hairdryer."

"They threw her out for using a hairdryer?"

"An American hairdryer, along with other matters."

"I don't like other matters. It sounds too much like things taken into consideration."

"She was in the middle of planning a rebellion but she was tittle-tattled just hours before it went off. She rigged the electricity so that it would fuse. She turned the water supply purple. And, Brian, the gas knob at one end of the school stove was going to heat a kettle at the other end. How would she do that?"

"The girl's a danger."

"She was sent home that morning. She didn't mind being expelled but she thought being called out in front of the whole school was unfair. As she says, half an hour later, she was on the train home and no one cared."

"It was probably to encourage the others."

"Brian, your clerk cadet has a good sense of fair play. She doesn't like to see people under-privileged and she can do figures like I've never seen before. You say 'em, she's added 'em up. I wouldn't be able to keep up with her fashion fads. She's a girl who's used to spending money."

"She's a good girl gone bad."

"You know that's unfair and it's not really you saying it."

"I don't know what croons means."

"Purring but like Al Bowly. And you do know; you're just being troublesome because you don't like the word."

"Can I trust her?"

"She'd rather get herself into trouble than let you down. A woman learns about another when they do Dickins and Jones together. Brian, she needs building up. Her father's tossed her into the real world and she's fallen on her face. More than once. If you can let her show you that she's at least half as good as she'd like to be, you'll put right an awful lot of wrongs."

"As big as that?"

"I think so."

"I saw a photograph of Evanshaw this afternoon. All the old Heads are lined up on the wall of the fifth floor and he was 1921-23. That was between our working together and his going colonial. You know, I felt proud, seeing him there." He kept his eyes closed. "Can you explain that?"

"Of course. You were very fond of him."

"Yes, I suppose I was. Did Faulkner give you a message for the girl?"

"She has a name, Brian. She says she'll have an answer for you tomorrow."

"But you did emphasise, she must keep it secret. No one must know what she is doing."

"I'm not going to answer your questions." She tossed the completed sock. "I'd rather keep your toes warm."

He opened his eyes. "The fire has settled. The streetlights have dimmed and the wireless is too weary to carry on."

"I liked Stanley Baldwin," she remarked.

"Are we talking about Stanley Baldwin?"

"I am, Brian. I'm sorry he's no longer your Prime Minister."

"Many people agree with you, my love."

"If ever I have a boy, I shall call him Stanley."

Storey lifted the modest brandy from the arm of his chair. "If ever? You're thinking of having children? You've got the girls." He regretted his tone. It sounded as if he thought she were greedy.

"I'm saying that Edward gave me the girls and, if I ever have children with you, I would want the first one to be a boy so that I could call him Stanley. Then he would grow up like Stanley Baldwin."

"If ever?"

"Yes, darling, only if ever." She turned, placed her head in his lap and whispered, "Do you know what I'm wearing under this gown."

He raised his eyebrow.

"Oh, no no no," she pooh-poohed, shaking her head. "No. I am wearing some very expensive frillies." She kissed his pyjamaed thigh. "Just for you."

Chapter Eight

It was a quarter to eight, when Debbie poked her head uncertainly around the door of the inner office. She calculated that her chief was on his third pipe of the morning - without coffee, without the fire being stoked and with no window open - so, she guessed, his mood was uncertain. "I did knock but you were thinking too much."

He jerked his pipe. "Come in, Cadet Holden. Come in. Take Sergeant Faulkner's chair."

She moved to the far end of the fireplace. "I'd rather have my own stool, chief. It's wobbly but ..." she shrugged "... you know."

"It's yours?"

"It doesn't cause trouble." She was clutching a folded memo between her fingers. "I've got the answer for you."

He leant forward, put his elbows on the desktop and took his pipe from his mouth. "Oh, well done, Cadet Holden. Let me hear it."

She hesitated. She watched the grey smoke curl around his ear before dispersing behind him. His face looked deep and weighed down by thought. "Only, you mustn't ask how I got it." She tried to chuckle. "You'd go spare, if you knew."

"Deborah, this is so important that methods don't matter. I want to know when the Chief Constable of the County, Detective Skelton and Mr Dominic Worth were in the same room at the same time."

She took a breath. "Tuesday morning. February 21, half past nine in the Chief Constable's office. Two superintendents were with them."

Storey nodded. "You telephoned Daddy's secretary?"

"Hmm." Like a nodding toy.

"And she telephoned?"

"We decided it wouldn't be safe to call the Chief Constable's secretary because she'd want to know why and she might even have told her boss. So, we thought, the typist - who agreed to take a peek at the diary as long as we kept it secret. She won't tell for fear of getting into trouble."

"Cadet Holden, that is very clever. Didn't I say you were clever? Please ask Sergeant Faulkner for half an hour of his time. Would you like to stay?"

She stood up and almost bobbed. "I have some other work to do, chief."

"Which is exactly the right answer. We're half way to making a policeman of you."

She turned at the door. "Thank you."

He raised an eyebrow.

"For calling me Cadet Holden."

"Oh, yes. Of course, it's only right."

When Faulkner came in, Storey tossed a spare tobacco pouch his way. "Have some of this. I want you to smoke for ten minutes before I put something to you. Cadet Holden won't let us be interrupted."

"Cadet Holden, sir?"

"We should allow her the credit of her rank, sergeant. Please, enjoy your Three Nuns."

Left alone, Debbie searched Harry's desk and collected his discarded ring of office keys. She stepped out to the corridor, locking the door behind her, and made her way to the staircase with large windows overlooking the town square. She climbed to the fifth floor, the most important flight in the building. The

Head Constable's suite was on the right and, on the left, three offices had been converted into rest and interview rooms (considered a waste by those senior officers who visited from larger forces.) Between them - a corridor of thick pile carpet, embossed wallpaper punctuated by portraits of the borough's alumni and sweet smelling plants in jardinières. Walking quietly, she hurried to the Watch Committee's room - the select - at the far corner of the passage. The door was open and she slipped inside.

She recalled the hallowed ground of the senior boardroom at St Mary's school. The long table so highly polished that no one could believe that any knees had ever been tucked beneath it. Glass fronted bookcases, a tooled cocktail cabinet and something strange which Debbie imagined to be a spittoon.

She trod over the carpet and knelt down at the corner where Mr Worth had died. Some of the carpet pile hadn't recovered its shaped since he had dropped here and the cleaners had not been able to disguise a patch left by his dried blood. Carefully, very slowly so that she wouldn't disturb it (a silly thought, she told herself later) she pushed two fingers forward to stroke the woollen tufts.

The door swung shut behind her, loudly - a loud bang - and although it had not been locked, Debbie was suddenly overwhelmed by a feeling of being closed in with the body. She shot backwards, bruising her hips as she collided with the table's edge, and twisted her ankle as she turned to her way out.

Miranda, the Head Constable's lady clerk, was waiting to bundle her up as she ran towards the stairs.

"Hey, now. What this? Oh, goodness! Quickly to the excuse-me."

"I want to share some ideas with you, Faulkner. Taken together they make a fairy story - we can't be any more sure of them at this stage of our enquiries - but like most fairy tales, you will find it chilling. Chilling enough, I think, to keep you away from church."

"I'm excused Sundays, gov?" "

"Yes, because the heart of the story is a truth that we'd rather not tell. Our pal, Williams, said that this case was bigger than we could imagine and, my god, he's right."

He waited for Faulkner to recharge the bowl of his pipe, sit back in the chair and draw deeply. The light from the window caught the side of the man's creviced cheek.

Storey began. "Two weeks ago, the Chief Constable of the county police suggested that it is time to make fools of the borough police. We should have a plan, he said, designed to demonstrate that Likely Storey, the borough's senior detective, is a bumbling fool. He said it with a smile on his face and he took the idea no further. After all, he might need to deny that he had been serious one day. He might need to complain that he's appalled that anyone should have taken his words and acted on them. But one of his senior officers knew the Chief Constable too well. He decided to win his superior's favour with a cleverly thought out hoax that, if it had worked, the newspapers would have loved to headline. He recruited a witness to complain to Inspector Storey that she was being haunted by spirits to the extent that she was able to walk through walls, put her hand in the flames of a fire and, ultimately, disappear without a trace. Why, Inspector Storey will even produce a letter claiming that this witness has crossed over to the other side. So far, how many people would this joker need to involve?"

Faulkner shifted in his seat. "Edith Winterton and Miss Langworthy. It sounds an elaborate hoax but you could spring it with just two players."

"They needed someone to answer the door when Harry knocked at number 239 on the Denning Flats."

Faulkner dismissed that. "Easy to fix. A neighbourhood like that. You wouldn't need to explain."

"And, come the day, guess what? Inspector 'Likely' Storey couldn't resist the intrigue. He dispatched a young constable to observe the place through the night and into the early morning. But, when it should have been all over, the plan began to go wrong. When Edith walked down the passage of Coldwater Place she was brutally murdered. The hoax no longer looked so funny. The link between the murder and the Chief Constable's comments may not be strong but the trail is certainly too short for comfort."

"Without the county boys she wouldn't have been there to be killed, gov, but there's nothing to suggest they had a hand in it."

Storey conceded with a barely noticeable dip of his head. "Matters grew worse, sergeant. Dominic Worth, who was there when the Chief Constable set out his challenge, later attended a regular meeting of the Poynton Committee. He sat next to me and noticed that I had drawn a cartoon of a nude Edith Winterton riding a grey haired tortoise on my minute pad which convinced him that the hoax had been triggered. He asked to meet Dougie Skelton in the Red Rose cafe. When Skelton said, 'We won't give him the money until we're sure he knows,' he wasn't buying information from a squealer, he was paying off a blackmailer."

"It won't convict them."

"No. It's enough for you and me but it's not worth putting on paper."

"Skelton finished the job by murdering Worth?"

"We don't know that. It's one matter to play a hoax and cover it up, it's another to turn into a killer."

Faulkner was cautious "The story leaves out any motive for murdering Edith Winterton."

"Quite right, sergeant." He stared out of the window for a few seconds. He asked, "How many of my loose ends it does it tie in?"

The sergeant brought his notebook from his pocket, found the correct page and read, "Why did Edith come to us in the first place?"

"Because Skelton told her to."

"Why did she go to Coldwater Place?"

"Skelton told her to."

"Why did she take your photo into the Red Rose?"

"Skelton again."

Faulkner objected. "No, gov. He didn't need that for his plan to work."

"OK. We're still looking for an answer"

Faulkner ran a pencil down his list. "What connects Coldwater Place, Denning Flats and Red Rose cafe?"

"Probably Skelton but I'm not sure why."

"Why would Worth take money from Skelton to keep quiet, then warn you off the next day? And why did Worth recognise Debbie in the Red Rose."

"I don't know. But that tells us why Worth was murdered. He would have told us why Skelton chose Edith and Miss Langworthy and why Debbie's presence put the conspirators at risk. And why was he so alarmed when he saw my drawing of Edith? That's another loose end. He knew all the answers. Yes, he had to be taken out."

Faulkner was itching to stand. He sat up, brought his feet to the foot of the chair and cupped both knees. "Gov, this is dynamite. If we are going to allege that the Chief Constable's ambition to take over our borough force has prompted two murders and discreditable behaviour in the county's detective branch, we'd better be damned sure of our facts. We can't even go to our Head until we've got the whole thing sewn up."

"It's worse."

"Too right, it's worse. The unworthy won't be sitting on their backsides while we creep behind them. They'll bloody ambush us, gov. Given half a chance, they'll turn it round and dump us in the wrong."

"From now on, it's all investigation work. Let's give ourselves forty-eight hours to learn all there is to know about Edith Winterton, Dorothy Langworthy and Dominic Worth. Pull Harry out of the murder team; I want to talk with him for an hour. I know the risk, Faulkner. Whoever we interview, we place is harm's way. But we've got to push forward. Tell Deborah I've got another job for her."

Part Two

Chapter Nine

J.P. would have nothing to do with the Red Rose restaurant so, two days after the murder at the borough police station, his sister waited for him at one of the three tables outside the Cat and Mouse, at the bottom of town. It was too cold to spend long on the pavement and Dorothy Langworthy was quickly irritated by the rickety tin table and the rickety tin chair made for a bottom that was much less than hers, but she saw the common sense of talking outside where no one would be listening at tables and passers-by, even if they were interested, would only catch a word or two. Not that the Cat and Mouse was a busy restaurant. It was on a corner at the bottom of the High Street - the last corner in town, people called it - where the traffic turned onto the trunk road. The cafe windows were never properly free of the smut from lorry exhausts.

She wouldn't be bossed around. As soon as J.P. started, she would say, 'I like Harry. He's a nice boy. I've seen him twice since and he's invited me for a day on the river and I'm going to go.' And when J.P. warned her that he was a spy for his police friends, she would say, 'So what? Let him ask questions. I know nothing about the killing of Edith Winterton.' She might add, 'who was a very nice person, like Harry.'

But when J.P. arrived with his ebony walking stick (it was only a lacquer coating, really) and his shoes which were more like slippers, he didn't want to talk about the experiences at Coldwater Place. He was wearing a black hat, like artists wear, but Dorothy was tempted to ask if anyone was due to be hung. "Everything has gone wrong, Dolly," he said in his breathy, theatrical voice. J.P. always spoke like he was reading a poem. "They've killed someone who had nothing to do with it."

Dorothy tuttered to herself and raised her eyes to heaven. She almost promised to say nothing at all, but to let him get on with it. But then he said, "Let's go inside and keep warm," which was a welcome idea.

The Cat and Mouse produced more steam than any cafe in town. It came out of kettles and urns, ovens the size of shoeboxes, and pipes that went up the wall behind the counter, and pressure steamers for suet puddings. J.P. swore that the Cat and Mouse had the only toaster in the whole world that emitted steam. "No matter what a man does in this place, progress is punctuated by whooshes and hissing and great burps like explosions."

"It's your fault. Are you going to order? You can't say anything when it's your fault. We could have gone to the Red Rose and sat with Bertie Williams."

"Dolly, how well do you know these people?"

Miss Langworthy's face brightened. "I had known Edie Winterton for years. We trained at the Co-Op together. Oh, she was a lovely woman - and a really lovely girl when she was younger." She sat up straight, raising her shoulders, and chuckled. "I could tell a story or two about Edie. If I had a mind to, of course. I won't be telling tales on the dead. I took over her job, you know, on the vacuum tubes." She looked at her brother's face and accused him, "You're jealous."

"Nonsense."

"You are. The tips of your cheeks have turned pink beneath the tufts of whiskers and that's always a sign."

The cafe-keeper's daughter, with strings of tawny hair hanging down from its grips and a pink overall hitched unevenly about her waist, arrived with her pencil and pad. "We can't do cheese and we've only one slice of bread pudding left."

"Two teas and teacakes," Dorothy requested primly.

"Teacakes?" Teacakes sounded a little posh for the Cat and Mouse

"Teacakes," said Dorothy, "and make sure the butter's lovely."

The waitress worked her sums on the back of the order slip. "That'll be two seven pennies. Pay when you've finished."

"Girls these days. She can't do what two seven pences make. Did you pick that up, Jean Paul?"

"And Mr Skelton?" he persisted.

Dorothy's startled face quickly looked about her. "Jean Paul, we're not supposed to mention his name. That was part of the promise."

"Dolly, I hardly think he's going to refuse to pay up. Not now. Not with two killings on his heels."

The girl returned with news that the teacakes could only be warmed in the toaster. "Our grill's out and we can't help it, Dad says, if the teacakes touch a little in the toaster."

"Oh, very well, girl." Dorothy shook her head. "Anyway, I don't know him at all. He was a friend of Edie's, that's all."

"Oh, Dolly, you really don't understand how mixed up this has all become. I wish you'd come to me at the start."

"And what would you have said! Don't do it, Dolly, that's what you'd have said." Then, because she didn't want to argue with him, she bent forward from the waist and said, "One thing, the teas in here are excellent. Edie's neighbour in the Denning Flats was telling me. Here's at the bottom of town and it's quite a trek back to the Denning, but she goes nowhere else in town for her cuppa. You wouldn't have thought it, would you? Not from a place like this. Now, sit back, Jean Paul. There's to be no more arguing and we're to enjoy our teacakes and teas."

"They left the Cat and Mouse tea shop at twenty five minutes to one. I followed them across the road at the main junction and we all climbed the High Street as far as Mulberry's." Cadet Holden was standing in the middle of the governor's office, reading from her neatly prepared notes. She was speaking in her best voice and was trying to breathe as her piano teacher had trained her but, for three days now, she had come to work with her hair pinned up and it was beginning to irritate. She had spent most of today walking up and down the steep hills in the town centre and, because she wasn't used to it, her shoes were pinching. And then, the inspector's office was always thick with stale pipe smoke - she could put up with that - but he kept the fire banked up and refused to open a window, so that the room was heavy with heat and Debbie always felt sticky where she didn't want to be.

Twice he had asked her to sit down but whenever she started to speak, she got to her feet, which prompted Storey and Faulkner to hide smiles behind their hands. "They didn't talk to each other once they had left the cafe," she reported. "I think their argument was like a huge family falling out for them." She went back to her record. "Miss Langworthy accompanied her brother to his bookshop in Friary Close but she didn't go in. She waited on the pavement while he opened up, then she returned to the High Street. She looked in shop windows until the Rialto opened at half past one, then she went in and bought a ticket for the back stalls. There was no one else in the queue and I made sure she had a couple of minutes before I went in."

"Was it a good picture?" Storey asked.

"Crooks Alley. I saw it last year. It's tiresome, second time around although the leading lady has nice hair. Nicely done, I mean."

"Film stars have time," Faulkner put in quietly, "and they don't do it themselves."

"Was she hoping to meet anyone?"

"I watched carefully, chief, and I'm sure she was there to pass the time, nothing else."

"Were you followed?"

Deborah shook her head. "Definitely not."

"Definitely, yes," Faulkner corrected from his armchair. "We'll each be followed from now on. County will have more men on us than fags in a packet."

Storey dipped his head. "The sergeant is right, I'm afraid. Did she treat herself? People often do in picture-houses."

"Sherbet toffees and fudge, but no chocolates. She left before the picture ended to catch the Number 4 back to Coldwater Place but you told me not to go near there, so I snapped off the tail and I came back here." She closed her notebook and said proudly, "Now, we know that Langworthy and Winterton were old friends. That's got to be important." She checked the faces of her colleagues. "Surely?"

Storey leaned over his crowded desktop. "Snapped off the tail?" he queried.

"Isn't that what you say? I'm sure I've heard it."

"It must be a Metropolitan saying. We won't have it in here, thank you"

"Sorry, chief."

"Sergeant Faulkner is our evidence officer. He'll tell you what we need next."

Faulkner sat forward, his knees parting - as was their habit - so that his hands could hang loosely between them. "If we are going to present a dossier to our Head, alleging that the county force meant to play a prank on us, designed to damage our reputation in the face of rumours of amalgamation, and that the hoax opened the way for two murders, we need to give our H.C. a watertight case to work with. We need to prove every connection, every step along the path. You've done well, Debs. That history been the two women is important. Now we need a statement from someone who knew about it, first hand. We need someone who'll swear to it."

"That's easy," she answered quickly. "The manager of the Co-Op where they both worked."

Storey shook his head, stood up and turned to the window. Seconds later, he was refilling his pipe.

"That's exactly what we don't do." Faulkner explained, "The other side will be watching every move we make. They'll take note of who we are talking to and that will give away the direction of our enquiries and how far we've travelled. We need to interview bystanders, people with no obvious connection to the case but who saw what was going on from a distance. Their statements will still be good."

"Heavens, it's like playing spies."

Storey came back to his desk, breathed out through the pipe so that his head was immediately encased in his grey tobacco smoke. A childish trick. "Exactly like that, I'm afraid. Very much, we are playing cat and mouse with our own fifth column. Cadet Holden, if you have finished your report, perhaps some coffee?" As she walked towards the door, he added, "And bring a proper chair for yourself."

"Please, chief, I like the stool. It fits my bottom."

When they were alone, he asked, "Did she really say that, Faulkner? Did she really say 'fits my bottom' in the hearing of a detective inspector?" Faulkner was grinning, face down and nodding. "And I don't much like 'Debs', either." Storey slumped back in his chair. He felt like sulking. "This thing's not just heavy, it's like a web." He cocked an eye to his sergeant. "A poisonous web? We'll find it difficult to make a case, you know that?"

"We're on the right track, governor."

"Are you sure? The stakes are pretty damned high if we fall short."

"We must expect the whole might of the enemy to be turned against us."

"What's that?"

"I'm sorry, gov. I was thinking of a phrase that Churchill put in a letter to my old boss. You've heard me talk of Whitey Baines?"

"Whitey Baines!" beamed Storey. "Good Lord, Whitey! A thinking man's detective, you know. I was with him when he interrogated the Bishopstoke traitor. I was there, sergeant, in the room with him. Good Lord and you're still in touch with him."

"He's in Whitehall now and has to deal with an almost daily tide from the crusty old soldier. But it's got a resonance, don't you think? 'The whole might of the enemy turned against us.' As a call to arms, I mean."

Storey was pacing the room with excitement. "No, I don't. Churchill's dangerous and reckless with nothing worked out. He's all rhetoric, man, and no argument. Bring back Baldwin, that's what I say. Janine was very fond of him, you know." He took his pipe from his mouth and cleared his lips. "In fact, too damned fond for safety."

There was a knock and a clatter - and a squeak that made Storey think of strangled mice. The threat of domestic commotion sent him back to his desk. "Watch that hat stand, Faulkner. It's going to tip."

Deborah was wheeling a portable wooden dinner wagon, complete with cloths and napkins, into the room. "I found it in Miranda's lavatory. She doesn't use it so I asked if we could have it. If there's going to be three of us from now on, I think we should have proper teas. I found some plates and knives and forks - and, if I can, I want to persuade you to use the serviettes."

Storey and Faulkner could think of nothing more out of kilter with the governor's office but they both knew that their latest recruit's bid for raised standards was beyond protest. Storey congratulated her on the acquisition of oven fresh scones, while Faulkner edged the saucer of crisp crackling to his corner of the display. "Sergeant," the governor remarked as he accepted a side plate of open sandwiches, "it seems that our conferences will never be the same."

Deborah returned to her stool by the fireplace. "I've another loose end for your list, skip."

"Hmm" A cough broke in the back of Storey's throat. "Skip?" He spoke with egg and bread in his mouth, moving it around and hoping that none of it would show.

"Oh, surely, that's countrywide. I've heard hundreds of coppers call their sergeants skipper."

"In uniform perhaps ..."

"I think we should allow it, governor," said Faulkner. After all, this was the first time he had tucked into crackling in the inspector's office.

Storey didn't comment further. He asked, "Why did Jean Paul, the fussily attired bookseller, want nothing to do with the Red Rose restaurant?"

"Chief," she complained. "That's the loose end I was going to say."

"You think we should question Williams again?"

"No," she said slowly. "No, he should be the last card we play. Once we show we're interested in Williams, the other side will move in to spoil things."

"Very good, Debs."

Storey cleared his throat and Faulkner corrected himself.

"Well learned, Deborah."

"And I know the best bystander witness."

The detective inspector walked around his desk to assess the remnants on the dinner wagon. He looked at his sergeant, "Are you hogging the crackling?"

"No, governor."

"I think you are, Mr Faulkner. It looks like Cadet Holden and I will have to make do with bread, butter and egg. Carry on, Deborah."

"A girl who ran out of the cafe in tears that night. She'd been the waitress in there. She was the only reason I asked him for a job. I knew she wasn't coming back. I don't know what that pig Williams did to her but I could tell that she was hating him, chief. I'm sure she'd give us all we want on the Red Rose."

"The scones were an especially good choice. You're in charge of the evidence, sergeant. Tell us where we stand."

"Dusty Ainsworth," he replied. "She cleaned the Co-Op for forty years and retired only in '35. She's kept in touch with the social club but has no obvious friendship with Edith Winterton or Dorothy Langworthy. She should be able to give us good evidence about their friendship."

"I like the idea of the Red Rose waitress. Follow it up." Storey pinched a chip of crackling. "I'm going to speak with Worth's widow and I'll do it by the duck pond." He collected his hat and coat and, with a call of 'Good hunting,' departed.

Chapter Ten

At fifteen minutes to six, the park-keeper was preparing to close. The ducks had been brought in for the night and the leisure dinghies chained up. Storey and Margot Worth had sat on a bench by the pond and chatted for half an hour. She was sure that folk would speak badly of her husband, now that he had gone. "He made so many enemies; you'll hear all that about him, and more, if you haven't already done so."

Now that the keeper was thinking of his supper, they began to stroll slowly towards the gate. "Are you sure you don't want a cuppa across the road?" Storey asked.

"You've been very kind, chief inspector."

It would have been petty to remind her that the borough police had no chief inspectors and no better than vain to mention that he was one of the few formal detective inspectors.

"I like that you've asked no questions."

"Oh, if there are any questions, they can come later, much later."

"But you want to know who murdered my husband?"

Margot Worth was a buttoned-up woman, short and squat like her husband, and given to wearing black even when she had no cause to mourn. She held her handbag with both hands and kept it close to her tummy as she walked. Each of her steps covered only half the ground of Storey's stride and he found himself wandering off-line to maintain pace with her. When she spoke, her little round mouth seemed hardly to move so that the words came out taut and clipped. "Catching the killer is what you're about, surely."

"I won't let you down, Mrs Worth."

"My husband was wise. He's a clever man who keeps his enemies quiet, Mr Storey. I'd like you to put that in a frame and put it on your wall."

He looked ahead; the keeper at the gate recognised him; in other circumstances, Storey would have made an exception and smoked a cigarette in exchange for gossip. He probably guessed that Storey was interviewing the recent murder-widow. Clearly, he was talking respectfully and the woman certainly looked widowed. "This isn't the sort of murder that remains unresolved."

"My husband was a blackmailer," she said.

They stopped. If they had more time, she would have led the detective to the ramshackle shelter overlooking the water garden. "Nothing big-time, you understand." She resumed their gradual progress to the park gates. "In fact, Dominic used to parade his modest approach to the trade as a virtue. Are you married, chief inspector?"

"Yes." He thought, I'm fifty four and my wife wants a baby, a son she can call Stanley Baldwin. Yes, she even suggests Baldwin as his middle name. I don't mind. After all, women are in charge of that sort of thing. Except, I'll be over seventy before the boy's off my hands and what good is an old dad to a young lad. How can I say that to her? Without sounding selfish and tired out? It would be like admitting that I'm no longer worth bothering with. And if it's what she wants, I want to give her a baby. I do.

"Would you tell your wife if you were a blackmailer?"

"I think I probably would."

"I hope so, chief inspector, because that would make you a good man, and I think you are."

She paused to open her handbag and revealed a black bound pocketbook which Storey mistook for a Common Prayer.

"I was going to chew things over. I wasn't sure what to do with it. But I am sure you're the man to take it."

"My love, I couldn't possibly ..."

"Don't be a fool. It's Worth's annals of blackmail. Whenever he returned from one of his appointments, he recorded the details in this ledger. Sometimes, I thought that it was his drive to fill this book that stopped him from reforming. I'm sure it will be of little use to you because he left out the names or addresses. But the killer is in that book, chief inspector, I'm sure of it."

That evening, after dinner, Storey pondered through the late edition, turning back and forth as he reflected on the opinions. By nine he was exasperated. The trouble with local politics, he was ready to say, was there was never enough of it. But Janine was quiet and he was happy wiggling his toes in his socks, having pushed off his slippers and rested the balls of his feet on the edge of the hearth. So Storey kept the grumbles to himself. Couldn't people see that neither motorcars nor narrow streets were a problem; congestion was caused by the lack of trunk ways. To damn the traffic and the town was arguing against reality. An early sign of madness, probably. And in these days of danger in Europe, did we want to devote three pages (three pages!) to readers' letters about a college's doubts over continuing to issue free ale to wayfarers at one o'clock each day? Storey's view? It was probably unlawful in the first place but he wasn't going to make a name for himself.

At half past nine he telephoned Sergeant Faulkner at home. "Worth had been blackmailing six people over two years. I don't have their names but he made one slip. He noted an appointment at the Red Rose cafe. So we've have it, Faulkner. We've got the connecting factor."

Faulkner, carrying his evidence in his head, asked if his governor had taken a statement to verify the document.

"Of course not, man. We were walking past ducks in the park. You think I'm some bobby on the beat, ready and prepared, eager to whip out his paper and pen at any moment? Are you eating toffee, Faulkner?"

"Home made Turkish delight. Sorry if it's a bit noisy. I'll bring some in tomorrow."

"Friday, Faulkner. I'm going shopping with Mrs Storey tomorrow. I shall enjoy watching Skelton's men waste a day's shoe-leather following us around."

The sergeant laughed. He said, "Your two foot soldiers will be busy with the Co Op cleaner in the morning and the Red Rose waitress in the afternoon. Do you want to meet up for lunch?"

"A good idea, sergeant. Mrs Storey likes the Talbot Inn on Thursday's. They do a nice suet pud; we'll ask them to save a couple for you. One o'clock?"

"It'll take some thinking through, exactly what this Red Rose tie-up means."

"Goodnight sergeant."

Storey prepared two beakers of Horlicks before returning to the fireside. "Worth was killed with a knife in the police station. Doors were locked as soon as the alarm was raised. Miller says that no one passed for a good twenty minutes previously and I've yet to meet a more eagle eyed desk officer than Sergeant Miller." He gazed into the flames. "The man's a fascist. I don't like him but that's by the by." He stood up, collected his pipe from the mantelpiece and warmed his rear end as he charged it. "Constable Brownsey was repairing a bicycle at the rear entrance. It was in pieces. No one could have walked down those steps before he'd moved all the bits. So, the killer was in the police station and probably stayed there. On the fifth floor we have only the H.C. and Miranda and an accountant who sometimes takes an office for sanctuary. But not on that day." He drilled his fingers on the pipe bowl. "This means that anyone could choose their moment at the top of the staircase and hurry to the Watch Committee's select without being noticed. We know that Worth was facing his killer and appears not to have defended himself. Not much, let's say."

But Storey had already lost Janine's attention. She looked up from her daydream and pleaded, "What times are these, Brian

Storey? How can we think of bringing a child into the world when the future's something we fear?"

He drew on his pipe and went up on the balls of his feet. "The thinker would say that stone-age man had the same worries and if he'd plumped for the decent thing to do, none of us would be here."

"But the thinker has no place here."

"Quite so," said Storey, drawing a line under the conversation. It was a mother's question, a woman's question, and he needed to leave her free to reconcile her instincts. "Do you mind if I go for a walk?"

"After your Horlicks, dear? It's usually pyjamas and bed after Horlicks."

He chose his best hat and a blue scarf that was too striking to wear in daylight. He stuck to his working coat because it had big pockets but pulled his oldest pair of brogues from the rack. He wondered, again, why Janine was so against him buying a walking stick but made up for it by lighting his largest pipe before stepping out into the street. It was a cold and noisy place where people marched with their heads down but always managed to avoid bumping into one another. It was smelly - a mixture of old veg, stray dogs and the lingering whiff of raw meat, not quite fresh, from the butchers' stalls. But when the evening lights came on in the shops and itinerants started to sing for people coming out of the pubs, when the women on the street corners caught his eye only to think better of it or when two or three youngsters were working up for a scrap in an alley; or when Storey was surprised by the headlamps of a turning car and was forced to wonder if it was deliberate, the High Road wasn't a dull place to live.

The young Constable Storey had honed his skills on streets like this and, walking out that evening, he hadn't lost the relish for straining every sense as he slowly plodded the pavement, catching snippets of half sensible conversations and keeping an eye out. He was heading, indolently, for the Grayling in Greek

Street but if he didn't get there in a quarter of an hour, he would turn back. And he wouldn't have pointed himself in that direction if the Grayling had nothing to do with Sergeant Miller and its rabid company.

He was two minutes from it when he saw the patrol sergeant at the crown of a junction directing P.C.s with a brace of prisoners into the waiting wagon. The boys from St Johns were there, wrapping more bandages around a twenty year old than you'd see on a professor's mummy. The lad wanted to tell anyone who'd listen that he was fit to walk home, except every time he tried to stand he ended up in the same gutter. It was a well managed incident - the lads who patrolled the Greek Street end of High Road had seen plenty of practice - so Storey kept his distance. He saw no sign of Miller but when he was walking away, through the back streets between the railway embankment and the coke stacks, he heard two louts congratulating themselves on the assault. The young victim, they were sure, had been taught a lesson that would discourage the others. 'Discourage the oats,' they called it without realising they had fallen between an English parody of French and an ignorant translation of the maxim.

"We got him away, all right," shouted one, wanting to play-fight some more.

But his comrade steadied him. "Rule One. You look after your own."

Storey didn't need them to say more. He knew that they were talking about the desk sergeant at central.

Ninety minutes later, Janine Storey lay on her side having folded her pillows into a ball so that she could look up at her husband without her neck aching. Whenever Storey read in bed, he wore his grandfather's cloth cap because it kept his head warm and, primarily, because it was so tatty that Janine wouldn't allow him to wear it elsewhere. Because it was heritage, he looked funny but strangely dignified. She poked the side of his great belly.

He grunted without taking his eyes of the page of his American thriller.

"One more time? To be sure?"

"Certainly not. We don't want twins."

"What if your wife is craving for you?"

"Janine, a lady does not crave. A lady deals with her womanly feelings in silence." He looked over the top of his spectacles. "You need a priest rather than a husband."

"I cannot believe that Brian Storey refuses me."

He took off his cap and glasses, turned down the corner of the library book and placed them all on the bedside table. "I shall make toasted egg sandwiches," he announced and swung his feet to the cold carpet. "All right." He explained, "Call me silly. But if we've been lucky, then surely further disturbance might queer the pitch." He twisted to look at her lovely face and he knew that she was already pregnant. He teased, "We don't want to flush him away. He's my eldest son."

Storey had carried the telephone and its pedestal from the hall and posted them between the bedroom door and the bed, but neither he nor Janine were ready for the shrill volume of its ring.

"They've arrested Debbie, governor."

"Send me a car." He was reaching for his trousers. "No, it will be quicker if I flag down a taxi. Where is she?"

"Drew Avenue nick."

"Don't wait for me, Derek. Insist that you're there when she's questioned." His head buzzed with different thoughts. "Derek, I need to work from our end. Stay with her, man."

Bastards, he said.

He was struggling with his legs. "I need to get this right, Jan." He grabbed the bedpost for balance. "What do you call it in chess, when you make a bold move to protect your king?" But he was on his way before she could think of it.

"Brian, take some tuck with you. Can't you wait for a couple of minutes?"

Chapter Eleven

The taxi driver wanted to talk. "What do you think of that bloke Anthony Eden? Clever man. That's as plain as a pikestaff but did he leap before he was pushed? As to my way of thinking, that's the question that changes all ways of looking at it. I'm avoiding Greek Street, captain. An hour ago they had traffic backed up as far as the old council house." He took the back route through town, climbing between terraced houses in narrow streets, redbrick schools and chain fences. As they turned left at a familiar sweet shop, Storey counted out his change, and would have been on his feet before the car stopped but the run down hill was bouncy enough to make him hold on. "Seven minutes, captain," the driver announced. "Quick enough to catch a train, eh? What do you say?" Meaning, surely it's worth a good tip?

The lad at the front desk hid his copy of the *Wizard* and snapped a salute as he leapt off his stool. "Good gracious, governor."

"Yes, son, and it's twenty past one."

"I'll tell the skipper you're in."

Storey asked, "Hasn't anyone told you that you should salute only men in uniform?" and disappeared into the lift.

He opened the door to the outer office and, using the light from the corridor to show him the way, walked through to his own den. It was damp and tacky and cold because no open fires were allowed in offices at night. He stayed in the dark and unbuttoned his coat, loosened his scarf and tipped his hat so that his scalp could breathe for a moment.

"And there's no coffee," he said to himself. He took the framed photograph of Janine and her girls from the pile of books and stood it on the top of his wooden filing cabinet. Then he collected Faulkner's portable lamp and threaded the lead between the furniture, through the door and around corners until he could balance it in Janine's place. He turned his chair around so that it was facing the window. He opened the curtain. Then, in his hat and overcoat and with his pipe in his mouth, he sat between the lamp and the window and reached back to switch on the bulb. Anyone watching from below would see his unmistakable silhouette behind the glass.

Over the years, he had practised sitting motionless, so that the guilty would look at his shape, two or three times, before deciding that they were safe. He was just a shape and not a person. Now, he tried to reduce the sound of his breathing and smoking, a move that seemed to exaggerate the other noises of a police station at night. The clanking of mops in buckets, doors left to close on their own, telephones ringing and sergeants forgetting how their commands might carry through an empty building. He knew that the nightshift would have found their own places, hidey-holes where they could disappear for twenty minutes, offices where they could occupy themselves with files of old cases that were neither normally nor properly available to them and those alcoves upstairs where illicit extra teas were brewed for those in the know. Canny coppers wore slippers in a nick after midnight, if they could get away with it.

He had soon smoked the remnants of an earlier pipe. Contentedly, he began the process as it should be done. He rubbed and aired each finger of tobacco before recharging the bowl. He used the tamper not to press or skew the tobacco but to bed it in and, each time, he checked with short baby sucks that the flavour could travel. And when he struck his Captain Webb, he allowed the first crackle of sulphur to dissipate before stroking the flame over the bowl.

He knew that Skelton would come. He had taken the girl in for questioning, sure that Storey would move to protect her. If the young cadet wasn't anxious enough to reveal what the borough team had been up to, the county man would make an explanation from Storey the price of the girl's release. But, unless he formally arrested her (and Storey was counting on there being no grounds for that) Skelton could play his hand for only a short time. And that was his mistake. "It's you," muttered Storey, taking the pipe from his mouth for a moment. "You're the one watching the sand spill through the waist of the egg timer. I can wait." He drew on the tobacco and enjoyed the flavour for a moment longer than usual. "I'm good at it."

His memory ran through the other times when he had enjoyed playing with time (though probably not so deliciously as tonight). Moments he had savoured as a suspect reconciled himself to having nowhere to go but to come forward and confess. Those nights -and sometimes a series of nights- when he had waited for a witness to return to the scene of a crime and, by putting right some inconsistency in their evidence, unlocked the crucial line of investigation. And now he was waiting for Skelton to come and show his hand. Hey, the county man was hoping for the same thing in reverse but he'd played it wrong. It was Storey whose silhouette at the window taunted his adversaries. Liking a fisherman on the towpath, he had all night to draw them in.

But when he heard someone scurrying about the outer office, he didn't poke his nose around the door to find a county detective. Janine had cleared a desk top and was spreading out one of the white tablecloths from the canteen.

"How's Debbie," she said without interrupting her task. "Do you know if she's all right?"

"Faulkner's very pleased with her. She's stonewalling. Faulkner says she's a star turn."

"You need to telephone her father." She was arranging cutlery and condiments. "Two of us, or more?" Then: "Don't worry. I shall run out of the way if I need to. Sergeant Meadows has given me the keys to the canteen and I'm not having you working through the night with no food. I've told you, Likely, it's bad for your stomach and it ruins the nerves."

He nodded. He was leaning against the doorframe and letting the pipe burn itself out. "I've just finished speaking to the Commissioner of the Metropolitan Police. It went surprisingly well and it is much easier to get through to him than I thought. I've asked him to show no interest - a stance he seemed disturbingly ready to accept."

Done, Janine slapped her arms to her side. "And now, you are waiting for news? I shall be back in twenty minutes with that Poulet-Basquaise you like."

He returned to his position at the window. He tried not to watch the clock on the mantelpiece and he didn't want to move in any way that suggested impatience. He reassured himself, "You'll come. You have nowhere to go, but here." He chose *The Mystery of Edwin Drood* from the pile of books, turned to page 48 and, having carefully slipped the bookmark between the last leaves, occupied himself with the master's visions of Rochester in the night-time.

When the telephone rang, he twisted to glance at the clock and stretched a hand across the desk. He allowed it to complete eight pairs of rings before he lifted the receiver and announced himself. "Borough police. You're speaking to Detective Inspector Brian Storey."

The message was delivered in an unmodulated stream which implied no response was required. He chose not to commit himself and replaced the instrument. The desk officer was circulating Mrs Storey's general invitation to a hot supper for all who were on duty in the station. The duty sergeant has declared an 'all hands'.

Storey was half way down the next page when he lifted his eyes from the book. "What's an 'all hands'?" he asked himself.

Twenty minutes to three. He could wait.

Then he heard someone in the outer office and something between a stoat with bunged up eyes and frog in a bad suit leant against the doorframe. "Every door's locked, Storey. Once you're in this place, you can't get out." Skelton, wearing his soiled blue lounge three piece, shiny with curled tips and stretched elbows and shoulders, was waiting to be asked in. His hat was old; Storey understood that a man doesn't like to part with his hat but when you're a character like Skelton, who looks ready to fall apart at any moment, a new hat's a good step to take for just a few shillings. His shirt collar had not been ironed and Storey didn't want to look down at his shoes. He felt like saying, 'You're a mess, Skelton. Find yourself a wife.'

Storey turned the chair and picked up a dry fountain pen from his blotter, as if he were going to write on something. "Janine is serving Bully-Bash in the canteen. Have you been up?"

The visitor screwed up his nose.

"It's a tomato stew with French chickens in it," Storey explained.

Skelton's lip curled to a snarl. "What are you doing, sat there like some ghost at the feast? You're putting the frighteners on villains for miles around."

"Have you told my cadet she can go?"

"Are you going to invite me in, you old bugger?"

Storey picked up the telephone receiver and started to dial. When it was clear that he was dialling a long number, Skelton barked, "What are you up to?"

"I've already spoken with the Met Commissioner. He asked me to keep him aware of progress."

Skelton ran forward. "I'll have you, Storey!" He slammed his knuckles on the phone, breaking the connection. Crouching over the desk, he turned his head to look up at Storey. The yellow light from the lamp caught his features and Storey decided that he had a face that smelled. It stayed like that, twisted and glaring, with stained uneven teeth and mismatched nostrils. Storey looked into the bloodshot eyes. The lamplight picked out the yellow and orange in the pupils and, for a bizarre moment, he realised that he was looking for fire in the eyes

Storey began to meaninglessly rearrange his desktop. "You have informally arrested -that's how I put it to the Commissioner- a member of my staff. I thought I would come here, keeping out of your way but readily at hand, and wait for you to tell me why?"

"She's led us a dance, Storey. My lads haven't been able to get a straight answer out of her."

"That's what we need. Straight questions, too. Try one."

"What was she doing in the Red Rose?"

"Waiting on tables, she says. I did wonder if I should caution her for taking part-time work when off duty. But then, you see, cadets aren't subject to the Police Act in the way that we are."

"She was working for you!"

Storey tried to keep his smile on the safe side of smugness. "I don't think she's said that and if she has, let me correct her."

Saliva bubbled at the corners of his mouth. "Play with me, Storey, and I'll have you peppered like a jugged hare for Easter."

"I am investigating the murder in this police station of Dominic Worth. We have a list of people we would like to interview but we've identified no connections with the Coldwater killing. I am required to report daily to my Head Constable who has undertaken to conduct any liaison with your Chief Constable. Should the two cases of murder cohere, I am sure that the superior weight and reach of the county force with demand precedence. Until and unless, I ask you not to further question my officers or cadet which, as you are aware, is beyond any protocol and likely to disrupt my own lawful and properly commissioned investigation." He dialled a second number and, within seconds, was saying, "This is Inspector Storey of the Borough. I'm with your Mr Skelton and he'd like you to release Miss Holden at once. Would you like a word with him to confirm? No, well, could you ask Miss Holden and Sergeant

Faulkner to pop into my office on their way home." He glanced at Skelton. "Do you want to speak?"

The man shook his head

"Mr Skelton asks you to carry on." He replaced the receiver. "I suspect they'll want to go over things. You're welcome to join in, Skelton, but you might feel uncomfortable."

Twenty minutes later, the inspector's wife was clearing the dishes of her chicken and tomato stew from the desktops and threatening to throw away the last slices of cakes if they weren't taken. Faulkner, who had been diligently recording notes, which would mean nothing to him in the morning, with the confidence of a Sherlock Holmes on a scent so hot that it scorched the ground beneath his feet, looked up and promised to take them home. He couldn't bear to hear threats of waste.

Storey was in the corridor, smoking and thinking alone, but nonetheless tickled by Deborah Holden's exhilaration. She wanted to eat, laugh, talk and listen at the same time and, when she couldn't, she made a mess of each of them. When he suggested telephoning her father, she responded mischievously, "I couldn't possibly speak to Daddy when I'm like this. Besides, he'll want to know all about it and then he'll interfere."

Storey came back to the office, slipping his smouldering pipe in his pocket and cupping a hand over it for safety. "I've a feeling that your father will play a big part in this affair before it's over."

She looked at him. "So you've been thinking it too. It was the one thing that was bothering me all through the questioning, but I thought I was playing too much of a detective. But then, if you think it too ..."

"Cadet Holden, you've got to give me some clue to what you're talking about."

She looked to Janine and then to Faulkner for support. "We've been thinking that Mr Skelton wanted to show everyone that we are useless so that the Chief Constable would look favourably on him. But look at him. He's a disaster. No police chief in England would offer him promotion and he must know it. So, I was thinking, it's more likely that his chief sent him out to do the job, because he knew ..."

Faulkner completed her sentence, "No one else was mug enough." He dropped his pen on the blotter. "Grief, governor, you're playing with fire." He got up and walked around the desk. "We've just shown them that we're up to it. We must expect them to raise their game. I'd say, we've got today and the early hours of tomorrow before we've off the case altogether." He congratulated Debbie with his best smile. "You look ready for a day in the fast track, even though you've had no sleep."

"But no less than you two."

Storey stepped forward. "But we'll be going shopping for shoes, Mrs S. I'll make sure we've time for that."

Falkner pressed his backside against the edge of a desk. "So you keep saying, governor. What have you got in mind, you old fox?"

But Storey gave nothing away. "Did anyone notice the best clue of the night? There was a hint of something that just might give us a bearing on the murder of Dominic Worth."

Janine was ready to carry the tray of supper debris from the room. "Of course, darling." She stretched up to kiss his cheek as she passed. "But none of us want to speak up before you."

"Does she know?" Debbie asked, looking from Faulkner to Storey, then running out to the corridor to see how far Janine had got. "She playing a game, isn't she? She didn't really notice anything?"

Storey shrugged. He had no idea. He explained, "The doors were locked so that the crew could muster in the canteen for Janine's bully-bash, yet Skelton walked in just the same."

"Which confirms," said Faulkner, "that there is a secret entrance to this police station and Skelton knows where it is."

Chapter Twelve

Dusty Ainsworth had not welcomed a commercial traveller into Number Thirteen since the terrible Mr Horne had lodged three nights with her (and that was back in '32), so when she saw the two characters at her back door she swore that they weren't coming in. Wearing her paisley housecoat, a man's large trilby spotted with bird droppings, and wellington boots patched with layers of pasted newspapers, she waddled up from the bottom of her garden, past the old fork stuck in the soil and the rake left where it had broken in two, past the compost in its rotting frame and the upturned wheelbarrow now sinking beneath the rockery, and around the bush which reached up to the washing line and covered the slab path. Miss Ainsworth was as wide as a house and twice as strong with three chins, and forearms like stone-age clubs. Her voice came up from beneath the pillow of her great bust and she used it like a growl. She carried a yard broom with six inch bristles.

"We want to ask about the Co-Op, Dusty," called Faulkner when she was still a dozen paces away. It had taken them twenty minutes to find the address. The pool car was parked half a mile away. If Debbie had been able to drive, he would have detailed her to bring it nearer. "Stay close," he whispered, "and be ready to run." He didn't like the way the old mare was handling that broom.

"That's your game, is it?" she said in a low rumbling voice. "You asked him next door what to call me so that you can start out all friendly. Well, it won't do." She came close and studied the sergeant's face. Her head lolled to one side, as if her good hearing was on her left and she wanted to pick up any whispers of what he was about. "You got any free samples for me? You won't sell anything to Ma'damme without you butter her up first."

"We're not selling, Dusty. I'm a policeman. Sergeant Faulkner from the Borough." Dusty Ainsworth wasn't a woman who would trust an offer to shake hands, so he kept them in his pockets and nodded towards the closed door. "I've got some questions about your years in the Co-Op."

Her face dropped and her eyes turned watery. At first, Debbie thought the cold was getting to her but the woman was used to being out in all weathers. She was as tough as old boots. On the other side of the fence, a back door opened and a neighbour kept an eye on things as she worked at her sink.

"Don't mind her," said Dusty. "It's about poor Edie, then? I'll help you all as I can but I've not seen the woman in years. The Red Rose tearooms, that's where you need to be. Talk to Williams in there and get him to give you the black on Dolly Langworthy's brother. He's the bugger in all this." She mounted the step. "Both of them, buggers, if you ask me."

"Please, Miss ..."

"Ma'damme, young lady, and make sure you say it right."

"I need to be excused."

"Well, there's no point in you going indoors and I can't let you into the privy because it's occupied. You wait there."

"Take them inside, you old crow," shouted the neighbour. "Her place is not fit to live in, that's her trouble, sergeant. She's frightened you'll get the council on her."

"The cold's getting to my tummy," Debbie explained. "I'm sorry, serge."

"You'd better let us in," Faulkner suggested.

"I've got a man in the khazi, tied up without a stitch on." She thrust the broom into Debbie's hand. "You want to go and poke him with this? He'd like you to punch his nethers with the bristle end."

Debbie's face turned brilliant. The old woman threw her head back and laughed, exposing the gaps between her remaining yellow teeth. Her mountains of flesh shook. The neighbour clattered saucepans like an exuberant cheerleader.

Faulkner, chuckling, put an arm around his cadet so that she could turn away. "I should have seen that coming, pet. It's my fault."

"She can't mean it." Debbie, cross with herself, fussed with her hair and straightened her coat collar. "She hasn't really got a man tied up in there, has she?"

"I've a half dollar that says he's fretting against you finding out."

The woman had left them alone.

Debbie paced up and down. "You won't tell the governor that I went red, will you?"

"You've done yourself no harm," he promised. "We need to stick with her. She knows more than we expected and if we can keep her talking, we'll get a statement that'll nicely sew up this end of the job."

Faulkner rubbed his cold hands together and moved to the side fence. The neighbour immediately shut the door and, from the safety of her kitchen, shouted, "Bloody coppers. We don't want you round here." A couple of passers-by looked from the front gate and shook their fists in agreement.

Dusty Ainsworth came out with three beakers of milky tea and sat down on the doorstep. Her round knees protruded from the drawn up hem of the housecoat, then flopped apart so that her elbows could rest on them. "Edie should never have been done in with such cruelty," she said quietly. "I'm sure I don't know one as wicked as to do that to her." She put her weight on the broom. "You needn't worry that Dolly Langworthy had anything to do with it. The pair were as close as two lovers."

"That's very helpful, Dusty."

She was chewing her lip and trying to tie her fingers in knots. "I don't mind telling you, I had a good cry when I heard. She was a good girl when she was working with Dusty. I never let her take a wrong step. If it wasn't for Dusty, she'd have got her heart broke in two."

"I need to write it down, Miss Ainsworth. You can tell me what to say."

She said, "You'll want to come in for that." She looked at Debbie. "Have you got a car she can sit in? She's got no need to come in my house. I don't want her in here. She's the bitch who stole Julie's job."

"No. It wasn't like that."

"We come as a pair," Faulkner said.

"Well, I don't want you looking around with your nose in the air, young woman."

And yet, the kitchen was as clean as any farmhouse scullery. Pots and pans hung on the walls where other homes might have found room for them in cupboards and the carpets had seen better days. And if the air was laced with a strong smell of vegetables and things brought in from outside, it was fresh and welcoming.

She was half way through the statement when she began to speak about Jean Paul. "You know him. He does the books in your police station. Regularly, once a month, he brings the old ones out and puts new ones in. He hurt Dusty more than any man's done. Albert Horn was different. He came here, full of promises. Old Dusty would do the garden and he'd make something of the house, that's what he said. He could bring money in, he said, and make it a home to be proud of. Sat with me in the evenings. Full of plans, he was. But in less than a week, he'd gone, taking all my rainy day money with him. Turns out, he picked up word of Madam Dusty's doings and thought he'd make a business of it. That's all he thought of me, sergeant. It's still makes me feel common to speak of it."

"A woman in your position needs to be careful, Miss Ainsworth."

"Watchful, sergeant."

"Who have you got in the privy?"

"You want to take a look at him?"

"Just quickly before I go."

"Jean Paul was after Dusty's soul. He made no move to court me in the ordinary way of things. Like, he tried to draw me in. With treats. And tea parties. He was very good with tea parties, Jean Paul, well he's that sort of man, you must have noticed. He liked it best when I told tales on Edie, harmless ones, mind. I'd never said anything that would hurt her. I think he liked to tease her. That's what it was about. And then he offered me money to do things. He wanted me to occupy gentlemen while he looked around their houses. Of course, he was very much taken with books but I was suspicious."

"How did he hurt you, love?"

"Seven pounds, that's what I was worth to him. He took it from that Sergeant Miller in the Grayling on condition that Jean Paul would fix it for me to play naughty with two of Miller's Nazi friends. They were going to tell on me, Sergeant Faulkner. It was all about getting Dusty into trouble with the magistrates. It breaks my heart when I think of how he wanted to dispose of me. Disposing, that's what he was up to. Like rubbish you no longer needs."

She looked at Debbie. "I know what you're thinking, young 'un. Dusty's the sort of bint who's been hurt by every man she's met, and you're not far wrong. But with Jean Paul, it was worse than ever. It was his way of doing it."

Faulkner took the statement slowly, announcing each step in the process so that his cadet could learn the way.

When it was over, the woman was weeping on the doorstep. "How could he do it? He was always so caring with Edie. Almost jealous of her but that needn't be a bad thing."

"She's best left to herself," Faulkner said quietly, sensing that Debbie thought it would have been right to sit with her. "I'll take a look at what's dreadful in the privy."

Debbie watched her boss step slowly down to the dilapidated shanty, open the door and take the quickest look inside. He was shaking his head as he returned. "A horrible sight. Captain Forsyte from the city council, though he's never turned up at the chamber like that. Cadet Holden, you'll see the worst of mankind in police work, bloated corpses, starving dogs and horses with no flesh on them. You'll see folk so wrecked by disease that you'll hardly reckon them human. And once your throat's choked on the smell of burning flesh, you'll never forget it. But you wouldn't want to see what's in that shed." He called out, "We'll leave you to it, Dusty Ainsworth," as he shepherded the girl back to the pavement.

Chapter Thirteen

In the Talbot Arms, which Storey always called a grey pub, folk weren't talking about the bad news from Europe, ministerial moves or even the prospects for the summer tests. The Talbot was a working pub. Golf, gardening and the devilment of manufacturing may have been the debate on the daily trains to London. And in the teashops and cafeteria, there were always the bus routes and the turnover of counter girls, if the picture papers could offer only mean fodder for gossip. In the town square the talk was of news headlines, next week's attractions at the picture-houses and what to do about too much motor traffic. But in the Talbot, men thick with ale and tobacco stuck to their yeoman heritage and talked of prices.

Farming was in a perilous state and if the small holding families had their heads above water, it was through no help from the government. A man could switch from dairying to lambs or, more likely pigs and poultry but if no-one wanted to pay good money for stock even the best made plans would come unstuck. Some put their faith in next season's weather but there was anger in the talk. The smoky air was thick with country oaths and more than one gloomy soul supped up his beer and walked out.

"The small man's dead," declared the stoutest figure, dressed up in his cravat and tailored overcoat, "and he'll not take his stead with him."

Inspector and Mrs Storey were sitting apart from the throng. They looked different. Storey had creases in his trousers and polish on his black shoes while Janine was unashamedly dressed for shopping. Their corner table at the back of the saloon allowed them to eavesdrop without being drawn into the arguments. But Storey paid so much attention to the local intelligence that Janine made a game of swapping from one subject to another without him noticing. "Are we waiting for Williams?" she asked.

Outside, the heavy traffic was pressing forward a few paces at a time as it tried to thread its way through the twists and turns of the town centre. Cyclists stumbled, pram pushers changed lanes and the motorcar drivers, always the least fortunate on mornings like this, counted the minutes before steam would grow up from their engine bonnets.

Thank goodness it was warm in the Talbot. Fires burned at each end of the long room and the old walls, two feet thick and broken only by small windows, kept the warmth in. The couple were happy to wait for their shepherd's pies with fresh carrots and said nothing to each other for long moments. Janine would have liked to look again at her new skirt from Dickins and Jones but this wasn't the place. Storey had bought a new loco for his layout; it sat, wrapped and tied with string (with wax over the knot, no less) on their little round table.

"It's rude not to invite him over," Storey remarked and was told not to go embarrassing the young policeman.

"He's been given a job to do, Brian Storey, and you'll not interfere." Janine went to her handbag for a fresh pack of Black Cats. "He's not bothering us."

Storey nodded at the county's constable, seated at the doorway. He had taken over from the off duty sergeant who had followed them from their flat to the town centre. Storey lifted a hand to acknowledge him and Janine delivered a sharp kick under the table.

The floor was a picture of gnarled boots, handcrafted sticks and well schooled terriers. Pocket watches were checked against the master clock above the fireplace and outstanding deals were settled with bold signatures. "How do they get big cheque books like that?" Storey grumbled. "Do you have to be a special customer?"

"If not Williams," she continued. "Jean Paul?"

"I shall ask our bank clerk when I'm next in."

"You wicked old thing. We're here just to keep our disciple occupied. I know what you're up to."

"Perhaps you have to be an especially favoured client?"

The pies arrived with carrots not only in the gravy but also freshly presented on a side plate. Grace Evans, who usually did school dinners for the juniors but set aside market day for her old employers in the Talbot, brought salt and pepper pots from the pockets of her overalls and mustard from the knot in her cloth belt. "Mrs Doughty says she hopes you'll be the first to try today's apple tart. She's been busy with it all morning, leaving me to get on with things that need to be done, which has been a godsend I have to say. You'll agree, Mrs Storey, there's no better feeling than being free of impudence under your feet?"

Janine smiled. "I agree very much." This was the kind of cooking that her husband would love. She caught him thinking, 'a break from the foreign influences at home,' and Storey, knowing he'd been found out, shared the smile.

When they were alone, he explained discreetly, "I think she meant impedance." Across the breadth of the timber-framed room, more pies and mash appeared from the kitchen and soon most of the assembly were tucking in, although the Storeys were the only ones who ate sitting down.

"We should make a regular thing of this. It's better than an hour with the newspapers," he said.

Sergeant Horndean from the Willow Place police station stepped through the door, looked around and, nodding to a couple of farming friends, approached the Storeys' table. The inspector was already on his feet and heading for the bar. "You're a brown ale man, if I've got you right, Horndean."

"That's very kind of you," he said to both, as Janine invited him to the chair she had been saving. "My Margaret asked to be remembered to you, Mrs Storey." He leaned forward, "She says I've got to make a good job of this or you and the inspector will think badly of her. Odd, the way wives think, you'll agree."

"Oh, my word, I agree," she chuckled.

Horndean had made sergeant early in his career but voiced no inclination to progress further. Fit, lean and six foot three, he was the bedrock of Willow Place with a memory that could place any piece of paper produced in the past twenty years. He was also the borough's walking authority on police history, a passion that would have crept indoors, but for his love of toy trains.

Storey was delayed by a white haired shepherd who was ready to fall off his stool and, for a moment, considered calling on Skelton's undercover man for help. The bowler hatted publican, with a white towel over one shoulder and a leather pad on the other, rescued the situation. With no fuss, the fellow was settled at the hearth of a log fire at the far end of the room.

"There's no upsetting the law in here," someone laughed good naturedly.

Storey placed the drinks on their table. "What have you got for me, sergeant?"

Horndean drew breath. "Not what you want to hear, governor. The Red Fire of the East is nothing to do with a jewel and much less to do with the old Orient, I'm afraid. It was 'the East' that had me befuddled to start with but once I got hold of it, the facts fell into place."

Grace was there, clearing the crockery and wanting to engage Janine in her chatter. The barman called her for fresh water and when she barked back, others around the room turned it into banter. When the fussed died down, Storey looked across and noticed that his watcher had moved from his seat by the door.

"It was a protection gang operating in Whitechapel at the time of the Ripper murders. Aberline was on to them. all right, but the thieves fell out before he could run them to ground. It ended with a bloody knife fight outside his own nick in '95."

Storey wanted to know where Skelton's spy had got to. Horndean was ready to tell the best of his story and Storey dared not risk it being overheard.

"You'll have heard what it was like in those days. Scotland Yard was there to be blamed for everything so Aberline was told to tread carefully. At their best, it was said the Red Fire could walk through walls but no one meant that literally. They had a reputation for disappearing, that's all. You know the rest."

"Well, I don't," protested Janine, keen for a good yarn.

Storey spoke over the lip of his beer. "Herbert Danvers-Wright was a constable in Whitechapel. He came to the county as an inspector before the war and would have brought stories of this Red Fire gang with him. His son is the Chief Constable Danvers-Wright we all love."

"It's no good to you," Horndean regretted.

"It's excellent news, sergeant. It's good circumstantial evidence that Danvers-Wright knew the background to the hoax. But I need more. Can you find out when Skelton first picked up on the East End's Red Fire? I need a witness, sergeant, who will swear that Danvers-Wright told the story to Skelton and I want it to be recent."

"That's all right," Horndean put in.

"Time's the trouble. I've none of it. Danvers-Wright will already be moving to spike my guns. I'm going to have to use all that I've got by the end of the day and, frankly, it's not enough. I'm so damn close."

"Governor, I reckon you're home and dry. All right, I've to fill in the gaps from my collection of newspapers. The *Police Gazette* has been useful and some old letters I collected from Aberline's people. But the core of the story came from old Captain Forsyte."

"Forsyte?" said Janine, warming to the story. "I've read about him. He's on the council."

"He's on Danvers-Wright's Watch Committee." said Storey, looking over his shoulder.

Sergeant Faulkner, on his own, was waiting for change at the counter. The sergeant took a taste of his pint and fished the collector's card from a fresh packet of twenty Wills before pocketing them. Storey watched the man's disappointment; he drawn another swap. He shared a word with an acquaintance and, avoiding a clutch of bus drivers in the middle of the floor, then made his way to Storey's table. "I left her with Julie, the former waitress at the Red Rose," he said before he was asked. "It's like a girls' camp reunion. They're getting along fine. Our Debbie will do better without me."

Janine was uneasy about that but Storey nodded; he was sure that his young cadet could cope with anything this town was likely to throw at her. Faulkner perched himself on a stool, "You've come up with some good stuff, Dennis? The boss looks pleased." He nodded at the package on the table. "I see you went for the Green Prince after all, gov."

The talk could easily have drifted towards model railways and Storey's new acquisition. Instead, the inspector brought his sergeant into the conversation. "Horndean's taken us forward, all right. It seems that our old friend Forsyte has an important piece of the jigsaw."

Faulkner twisted his head to look around. "Skelton's men aren't following you. governor? I can't believe they've given up."

"Our disciple's managed to lose himself, which gives Mr Horndean chance to tell us the best bit."

The sergeant from Willow Place coughed and inched himself closer to the little table. "Captain Forsyte was waiting in an ante room when the chief promised a thousand gilders to the officer who could deliver your head on a plate."

"He heard him say that?"

Horndean nodded. "I questioned him, Mr Storey, and he swears that the chief actually used the term 'gilders'."

"Why would he say that and not pounds, or even shillings?" Janine asked.

"In case he ever needs to pass it off as a joke," said Storey. "He could argue that it shows he wasn't serious."

"But Forsyte can take us further," Horndean continued. "He was there when Skelton hung back after the meeting. He heard the chief talking about the Red Fire of the East. But the old boy won't give you a statement. I can promise you, he won't."

Faulkner swallowed hard. He threw his head back and laughed. "Oh, he'll give a statement, all right. If we're waiting for the good Captain Forsyte, we're as good as done and dusted."

Debbie and Julie walked gaily along the river bank which fingered its way from the bottom of town to the unkempt verges of meadow and farmland. They had run out of footpath and, Julie leading the way, battled through bushes and fallen branches. Debbie kept close behind, looking only at her friend's rear end as they shouted to each other. Julie was better dressed for the task with slacks and a jumper and Debbie wondered if she looked more like a boy than a young woman.

They didn't kiss each other's lips until they were resting on a clear patch of the bank, watching the water trip over a weir which a colony of beavers had made the year before. The noise from the town seemed far away. The kiss had been so unexpected that neither side knew what to do next. Julie rested her head against Debbie' shoulder. Neither spoke and she soon stretched out so that her head was resting in Debbie's lap.

"We ought to be aviators together."

Debbie was lightly twisting strands the of girl's fine hair between her fingers. "We don't know how to fly."

"We could learn."

"We don't have any aeroplanes."

"We'd only need one. We could take turns as the pilot and fly all over the place. That's how they do it. From one hop to the next."

Debbie said softly, "You're dreaming."

"Your father's got plenty of money, and you must have uncles and grandparents. All the aviators get other people to buy their planes. I've read about it."

They were miles from anywhere. The water was making a rippling sound and they had no idea of time. The conversation had run its course and they gave way to their feelings. So quickly that neither could explain what was going on, they were lying full length on the rough grass, kissing and exploring urgently. Julie wanted to go further but when Debbie insisted, "We must stop," she relented.

"We're wrong," Debbie warned.

"I know. I'm sorry."

"No, please." She collected Julie's hand and held it firm.

Fields away, a little aeroplane was fighting to gain height and, without a word, the girls were thinking of aviators again. Julie pulled herself away, folded her knees up to her chin and wrapped her arms around her shins. "You only brought me here because you want to ask questions."

"But we're friends, aren't we?"

"Even though I told Dusty that you'd got me the sack? I wanted to get her cross with you."

"It doesn't matter."

"But you won't kiss again until I've told you."

"I will." It was difficult to say and she'd had to brace herself before the words would come out. "Am I pretty, Julie?"

"No," she teased and Debbie gave a playful poke to her ribs. "I think you're for scoffing. You're a scrumptious cake that needs to have the cream licked away and all the jammy bits sucked out and then eaten in goods mouthfuls that must be chewed twelve times each before swallowing."

"God! That's so rude!"

Julie turned her head so that they were face to face. "I'd have to take your clothes off first."

"Stop it."

But Julie wouldn't turn away; her eyes were so demanding.

Debbie whispered, "I do want you to," then covered her face and rolled onto her tummy so that she wouldn't see Julie gloat over her embarrassment.

"Come back, Sooty," Julie laughed.

"No I won't."

"Do you hate men like I do?"

"No." Debbie's voice was still muffled; she spoke into her hands with her face hard against the ground.

"I hate men like Williams and Skelton, and Jean Paul most of all. I can't look at him without feeling him wanting to touch me. He's got fingers like probes. Williams wanted to leave me alone with him, that night in the Red Rose. I knew that he was going to do it, whatever I said, so I ran off." She sighed with just a trace of impatience. "Come on, Sooty. This is what you want to hear. Sit up straight and listen."

But Debbie wanted to get away. If she left now, before things went too far, she could convince herself that these thirty minutes hadn't happened. "I want to walk back. I'm late already. People will worry."

Julie threw herself back on the ground. Her laugh seemed to shake the leaves. "Well, that's one hell of a policeman!"

"I don't care. You can laugh all you want."

"Don't be such a baby!"

Debbie was on her feet and dusting herself down. "Good-bye, Julia."

"Oh, yes, 'Good-bye, Julia', " Julie called as Debbie walked off. "You're not fooling me, Sooty. What are you scared of? Scared of yourself, that's the truth!"

She followed her, teasing her with more information. "Dommie Worth heard them planning something." But Debbie didn't turn around. "Those two women were always in the cafe together," Julie shouted, "and he heard them talking about a joke that Skelton wanted them to bring off. I don't know what it was, but you do. That's what you wanted to ask me about."

Debbie was walking so fast that the backs of her legs ached. If she pushed herself any harder, she would break into a run.

The girl didn't care who heard. She was yelling like a spoilt child. "Worth set up a meeting with Skelton. He said he'd see them down at the docks. He was going to tell them to pack it in or he'd tell on them. Do you think that's why Worth got murdered, Mrs Policeman?"

Debbie didn't turn around. Julie gave up following her and finished the story, more to herself. No one was listening. "Williams wanted to spy on the meeting. He wanted to find out what Skelton was up to so that he could use it against him. Do you think that's it? Do you think Williams had to keep Worth out of it because he wanted the action for himself?"

By now, Debbie was thirty paces ahead. She was already passing the backs of houses and the factory fences.

"I hate them, Sooty!" The girl shouted as loud as she could. "I hate every one of them. I hate what they do to us."

The warden in a factory wagon park stuck his head in the air to listen. But all he could hear was the noise of the aircraft engine and he started to step round in circles as he searched for it. A woman in a housewife's smock came out to her back step and listened for more. She decided that the shouting had been kids, larking about. She went back indoors.

Julie had already collapsed against a wooden stile. She slid down to the mud, sobbing, wiping her tears with the backs of her hands. It felt like her last breath as she crowed, "You don't know, Sooty. You won't listen. Please, listen to what they've done to me."

Storey stood beneath the porch of the Talbot Inn and sniffed the good afternoon air. "Will she give us a statement?" he asked as he put his gloves on.

"No!" Debbie snapped. "No, and it would be too complicated for me to do. Sergeant Faulkner would have to take it down. And anyway it's a waste of time. She even made me promise not to tell anyone. She said it had to be kept secret." A little voice told her that she'd gone too far; she had no need to fib. But, once said, it would make too much fuss to correct it.

Faulkner was leading them towards his pool car.

Storey smacked his hands together and took another deep breath. "No? Well, you'll have to write down what she said." "Half our evidence is hearsay so a little more will make no difference. What do you think, Cadet Holden? Shall we have a brisk walk up the hill? Faulkner can take Mrs Storey home so that she can try on that new skirt. She's desperate for it. Desperate. What do you say? You and me, and a good walk up the hill."

He shook Faulkner's hand. "We've got it all, you know." Everyone could tell that the inspector wanted to cheer. "It's just a matter of writing it up."

Sergeant Faulkner and Debbie staked their own territories in their inspector's office, where the coal fire burned through the night. The outer office became the 'cold room'; here, Faulkner opened his master file in virgin buff covers but not a single piece of paper was tethered to it without first passing through his hands. He checked its evidential value and, back in his corner of the governor's office, he ticked off every point in a rough and complicated log. He laid this log, which grew to look like a scrapbook, at his feet and neither Storey nor Debbie risked touching it, even when he was out of the room. He marked everything that needed corroboration, every loose end and every orphan (a fact left dangling with nowhere to go). Between one and two o'clock the sergeant and the cadet worked so well together - they were thinking in unison and developed their own shorthand way of talking - that Storey withdrew from the reasoning and took on a role resembling 'cook and bottle washer'. At one stage, he carried fresh coffee into the room and found the cadet seated at his desk, diligently handwriting her first ever statement of evidence. And when Faulkner took her through it, pointing out the importance of sequence, time, and place and how the investigator's initials after important facts impressed the local magistrates, there was something of a father and daughter in the tone of the tuition.

The night-duty inspector, usually at home and on-call after two o'clock, sensed that things were afoot and kept himself on duty. He even poked his head into the 'cold room' and offered an extra pair of hands. But Storey assured him that no arrests were imminent.

Soon, the log at Faulkner's feet was scarred with so many asterisks, lines, arrows and brackets that it looked ready to force itself into the third dimension. "It needs to be right," he muttered under his breath. "Check, double check and check again." Now and then, a niggling doubt would play on his mind and send him scurrying to the cold room and the master file. But as the night passed through the doldrums of three and four o'clock, Faulkner grew in confidence. His master file was emerging as a docket to be proud of. "We've got belts and braces where we need them, gov, and good circumstantial evidence to make it all believable."

They broke at four-thirty for strong 'coppers' tea and thick slices of new bread toasted on the open fire, with butter knobs and marmalade purloined from the canteen kitchen. Debbie folded herself, cross-legged on the hearthrug while Storey reclined behind his desk and watched the reflected glow on her face. It was Faulkner who was doing the work now and, as he licked the last of the butter from his thumb, he announced that he would retire for one last thorough look through, checking that everything was numbered, signed, dated and cross referenced before making a presentation to the others. That would be their last chance to pick up anything he'd overlooked.

Chapter Fourteen

Miranda Millicent, the Head Constable's lady clerk was in before seven. "I've told him that I want to be away at three o'clock," she explained as she arranged her desk for the day. "We're rehearsing Puccini tonight and Frau Heffner's such a tyrant that some of us want to limber up before she sets eyes on us."

"You'd better cancel," said Storey. "You're in for one of those days, Miranda. By lunchtime, you'll think you're doing aerobatics over Eastleigh aerodrome."

She adopted a mock scowl as she eyed the file that Storey had tucked close to his chest.

"I want the Head to give twenty minutes to this early on."

"Hand it over," she sighed. "I'll put it on his desk before I fetch his breakfast. I've found that's a good time for him to concentrate on something new. He wants to visit Willow Place this morning?"

"You might as well call that off too."

She was trying not to be cross with him. She asked if Janine had reconsidered her refusal to join the amateur operatic group. "She'd be a real asset. She's got such a good voice and we all know how she can act. I saw her role in *Hay Fever*. She must know that she's good; she got a mention in the County Press."

"Janine will never work for a German, Miranda. She's carrying too much to let go."

"Frau's not a German! Frau's our nickname for her, the way she carries on. But Janine could handle her."

The detective offered a deal. "You keep everyone out of the Head's hair while he reads my papers and I'll have another word with Jan."

She prepared to enter the Head's office. "You can wait in the accountant's den, if you like. He's not been in for a week. Or there's the select? He's put a bar on anyone but you walking in there. Go on, and I'll bring you a cup of tea once the boss is settled."

The select was cold. Storey stepped inside but stayed at the door and pictured the murder. Worth had been alone in here and not expecting his killer. The culprit had, probably, gained entry in the same secret manner which Skelton had used a couple of days ago. They had stood face to face. If there had been an argument, it wasn't enough to alert Miranda or the Head Constable, only three doors away. So, a brief exchange of words before Worth was stabbed in the chest. He fell backwards against the wall and was close to death by the time he dropped to the carpet. The attacker made his hurried escape without anyone seeing him. With his hands in his overcoat pockets, Storey went to the far window overlooking the town square. He knew that his thoughts on the case had been trapped by his obsession with building a case against the county police. He needed to free himself from that. He tried to reduce all the evidence - the statements from Captain Forsyte, Dusty Ainsworth, Jean Paul and the others - to one simple storyline. Eventually, that was how he would recognise the motive and twenty years had taught him that motive was, always, the key.

When he was called to the Head's office, he found the old man sitting in a chair turned sideways to his desk, so that he could cross one knee over the other and study the dossier in his lap. He had started a cigar, but it burned unmolested in a pen tray with a long finger of ash balanced at its tip.

"God man, do you live in that coat and hat?" He didn't look up. "Hang them behind the door and drop yourself in an armchair. You won't think properly until you've got your pipe going; get on with it. God man, this is dynamite."

He reached the last page but gave no response before returning to the beginning and absorbing it all again. Sometimes he sucked through gritted teeth, sometimes he tossed his head. His free foot went up and down like a ticking time bomb. He tapped a fingernail on one statement - Storey leant forward. He thought it was Dusty's. "Yes ... this one," and he studied it word by word.

Then he pushed himself even further back in his chair and ran his fingers through his black, greased flat hair, making a comic mess of the short back and sides. "This is an astounding piece of work, Storey. Well done."

"Sergeant Faulkner is the best evidence officer I've come across, sir."

"Yes, he has a talent for it, certainly." He smacked the dossier on his blotter. "Danvers-Wright is a bastard." He hauled himself out of the chair, stood at the window, said it again, then turned around and pressed his backside against the sill.

"An astounding tale, inspector, but what do I do with it?"

Storey knew that his boss wouldn't enjoy hearing the strategy but the stony look on his face said that he was ready for it.

"That man needs kippering. Come on, Likely, tell me what to do."

"Bring in the Yard."

"Ah, hell, man."

"Ask them to head up the Worth enquiry and put that file in the Commissioner's hands as a briefing. Sir, this is the first murder that's been my show. I won't like losing it any more than you will, but bigger fish need frying."

The Head Constable saw the cold sense in Storey's approach but he grimaced at the notion of losing a murder case.

"As soon as the Yard get their hands on it," Storey continued, "they'll combine the two enquiries and the whole thing will be opened up. County have done nothing with the Coldwater Place killing. They've got no room to move without causing trouble indoors. They wanted to show that we're fools. If we bring in the Yard, we can turn the tables on them." He considered calling on Evanshaw, Dodridge and the others to bring weight to his argument but decided to allow uncomfortable silence to do its work.

The Head Constable wiped his face. "Faulkner's minute on the half-sheet. Is that your doing? It's the killer."

"Our enquiries have been building at a pace. Faulkner's always been one to keep the ball rolling."

"If I pass this to the Commissioner, he'll spill it to the Home Secretary, you know that? The county chief will have to resign and we'll all be lit up like Crystal Palace on bonfire night. What about our own backyard? We've got no dirty secrets, have we? Put the word out, Likely, I want the place swept clean. Are we close to solving the murder in the select?"

"Sir, every sinew in my body says that the thing's going to break in the next couple of days. You know how I work. I ring the suspects with snipers and wait for villain to show himself. But I can't work it to a deadline."

"But we can show we're on top of it, can't we? We mustn't look like country bumpkins. What about an arrest? Something initial, a beginning? Things would look brighter if we had a body in the cells."

"I'll make sure the pot's boiling. We won't be embarrassed."

"That Danvers-Wright's a bastard."

Storey pressed. "I can be on the 8.53 to Waterloo. We'll use Cadet Holden to smooth the path to her father's office. Danvers-Wright will be discredited before lunch."

The Head Constable gave a curt nod. He stood over his telephone as he spoke to his lady clerk, smoothing his hair into place. "Get onto the station manager. I mean the railway, love. Tell him the 8.16's not to leave until Inspector Storey's on board."

Breakfast was waiting in the ante-office, the fire needed stoking and the town clock was striking eight o'clock.

"Get your hat and coat, Likely. Good luck."

He sat down at his desk and dialled a single digit. "I want a person to person with the Met Commissioner."

Part Three

Chapter Fifteen

The break came sooner than Storey expected.

He was striding across Waterloo's concourse, with his brown attaché case under one arm, and already fingering change for the taxi in the other pocket, when he was approached by a Met sergeant.

"Inspector Storey?" he enquired with a salute.

It's unnatural, thought Storey, all this saluting officers without uniform.

"I recognised you from Miss Holden's description. The Commissioner hopes that you'll meet him in the Reform. I'm to take you straight there."

It was easy for folk from the sticks to be overwhelmed by the capital and certainly no provincial detective could brush shoulders with the Met without realising that policing London was a different kettle of fish. But Storey always felt safe here. People seemed to know their business and he enjoyed being physically close to the centre of power. Whenever he strolled along Whitehall, he was impressed by its importance. Unlike Miller and his cronies in the Grayling, unlike Janine who had more reasons than most to be a sceptic and, yes, unlike Faulkner and H.C., he believed that the chaps in Westminster got things right more often than not.

But things were happening back home.

At ten o'clock, while Storey was sinking into a sumptuous leather armchair, accepting a dry sherry and wondering if he had shown bad form by refusing a cigar in favour of his own pipe, Sergeant Faulkner was trying the inspector's chair for size and waiting for a fraught army captain (retired) to stop fidgeting in the easy chair at the hearth.

He was a long man with shoes which would have been three sizes too big on any other man of his height. He had a tawny complexion, ginger hair and ginger whiskers which he'd encouraged to grow forward on his cheeks. He looked unfed. Faulkner decided that he probably drank too much.

"It's time to make a clean breast of matters," he said. He brought his gloved fingers together, making the shape of a church, and rested his weighty chin on the steeple. "It'll finish me in this town, of course. I'll have to resign my interests and take up gardening. Gardening's a solitary pursuit for those cast out."

"I shouldn't worry, captain." Faulkner elaborated cynically, "I've found that your circles are likely to close ranks. Whatever your embarrassment, it will be kept quiet. I've never been one for withdrawal. Throw a big party, that's my advice, and damn those who don't turn up."

"Yesterday, you saw me in Miss Ainsworth's outside toilet."

"I've written nothing down," Faulkner assured him. "My inspector knows and our clerk cadet, of course, but it's gone no further."

"But it needs to, sergeant. This whole mess has been starved of daylight for too long."

"Please smoke if you wish."

He patted his pockets and brought out a cheap brand of cigarettes. "Sergeant, I have the best motive for murdering Edith Winterton. The wretched sow had been my blackmailer for five years." He lit up and drew in heavily. "You'll understand if I speak roughly of her? She's dead and the world's better off."

Faulkner said nothing but lifted a noncommittal hand.

"I called on Dusty, the first time, at the end of the war. So what's that?"

"Twenty years ago."

"She's a very kind woman, not given to harsh judgements. I've always thought our contract worked well. But not so, Edith Winterton. She blundered into one of my visits -five years ago, as I say- and she was asking for money within the week. On the night of the murder, she wasn't expecting me. I'd decided to have it out with her. I meant to tell her that she's taken enough money off me to last a lifetime and I was prepared to face up to her threats."

"Captain Forsyte, the law takes steps to protect the victims of blackmail. My inspector views it as one of the worst crimes in the book."

"Well, he might. The distress it causes can't be counted. I had been through enough of it. But I saw your young detective observing from the street. He'll tell you that I even approached him and we had a cigarette together. He'll tell you that I walked away and left him to his business."

From the start of the interview, Faulkner had accepted that he would be told only half the story. Men like Forsyte needed to develop a trust in their interrogators. "I'm not going to take a statement. I want you to think about what you've told me and, when you're ready, we'll set down all the details. Go about your day in the normal manner. I think you might be called to an emergency meeting of the county's Watch Committee this afternoon. Take part. People will be watching you and I don't want them to suspect any change in your position."

Forsyte pressed hard on the arms of his chair and stood up. "You talk as if things aren't over for me?"

Faulkner offered his hand. "If you didn't murder Edith Winterton, I see no reason to include your evidence in the investigation. Captain, you're in no worse position and a good deal more comfortable than many men who've past through this office. But when word gets out that you've visited this police station, our county colleagues may want a word with you. Go carefully, Captain."

"When this is over," the Commissioner was saying as he dabbed a white napkin at a slither of white sauce on the corner of his lips, "I'd like you to find a place on your staff for my daughter."

"She'd be wasted," Storey cautioned, hoping that this was mere talk at a lunch table and wouldn't develop into an order. "Mind, my wife's picked up that Deborah's got an eye on the WRNS which would be twice the waste. Your girl's very talented, Commissioner, and I mean more than just skilled. She needs to be challenged; that's how she'll grow. She'd be a credit to the Met, I can promise you."

"You really think so? I've told them not to bring that sorbet you ordered, by the way. You'd be disappointed."

In the Reform Club? Storey wondered.

"The treacle pudding is difficult to master with these damned silly forks they give us, but worth the effort."

In the Reform? I lunched at the Reform and had treacle pudding?

The Met Commissioner was a gentleman whose company Storey could enjoy while knowing that he could never match his savoir faire.

"I've never shown her the respect she deserves. She's our youngest - she always has been, of course, and always inclined to be difficult. A little more effort on both sides, do you think?"

"There's going to be a war, Commissioner."

"Undoubtedly and you boys in the south will be in the thick of it."

"And Debbie will work well with spies."

That took the father by surprise. "As good as that? I know that Max Knight's looking for women." He studied Storey's face for further comment and didn't change his expression as he asked, "You know why she was expelled from her school?"

Storey wanted to say it was none of his business. "St Mary's? It has its own trains, I believe, and takes in daughters of kings and queens. My wife says that Debbie was caught with an American gadget."

The Commissioner laughed. He recalled his discussion with the headmistress. "Yes, it was very good of the school to find such a curious excuse. It makes a good yarn, don't you think? Mr Storey, she was thrown out for having an affair with one of her mistresses." He laid his knife and fork down for a moment and mouthed each word explicitly, "A torrid affair."

He had called a waiter to the table and whispered instructions. "Yes, I know it's against the rules," he insisted, "but that's part of the fun. Is old Withers in? He likes to complain about my habits. He says I'm a heathen."

He waited until they were alone before asking, "Do you think you could talk with Deborah about it? I'd like to know what really happened. How far things went, things like that. Or your wife perhaps? I gather she's a great help for you."

Storey said, "I've always thought that Inspector Bucket was my sort of detective. I'm always happy to take a leaf from his book."

"Bucket?"

"*Bleak House.*"

"Oh, good gracious, yes. Yes, and Mrs Bucket, of course. My word, yes. I can see where you're coming from. God, I'd like a man like you in my East End."

The steamed treacle pudding with fresh cream and ice cream was everything the Commissioner had promised. He inclined towards Storey, only an inch or two, and confided, "We're going to take cheese in the card room. It's a damn sight warmer than here and I want to go through that dossier with you. You know what you've got there? I'm down to see the P.M. at three and I want all the facts at my fingertips. Have you ever done Downing Street, Storey?"

"No, sir. No, I can't recall a summons to Downing Street and I'm sure I'd remember."

"You'll get no further than the ante rooms. The P.M.'s a dyed in the wool snob, I'm afraid. Probably no bad thing. I'd like to have you on hand. Say no, if you've not got the time."

Skies cleared in the afternoon and when Storey, ignoring the newsvendors' cries of bad news from India and resisting the temptation of a cup of tea beneath the departure board, offered his ticket for punching at the platform gate, he looked forward to a reflective journey through the capital's hinterland. He had deliberately chosen a slow train. He had promised to meet Scotland Yard's detective as soon as he got back to the borough and the slow stopper granted him an extra forty minutes before formally handing over the reins. Even now, as Storey hurried the length of the platform, seeking a compartment to himself, Faulkner would be giving the new man his best briefing on the Winterton case.

He found his seat in the front compartment of the first carriage and, not for the first time, tried to calculate if this was the safest or most vulnerable part of the train. He closed all the blinds and switched on one of the overhead lamps. It worked, then faded away like a worn out battery. Storey didn't interfere as it tried again, flickering and popping and, feeling sorry for itself, offering a light no brighter than a Christmas torch under the blankets. It wasn't until he sat down that Storey realised how tired he was. He hadn't slept for two days and nights.

A hurried phone call from Scotland Yard had given him an outline of Forsyte's evidence. The tailpiece had been Faulkner's telling assessment, "I had him for an hour, governor, and he never denied murder. And, governor, I never trust a man who keeps his gloves on during an interview."

The *Evening News* was folded on his knee. He took in the headlines but knew that he wouldn't read it. He'd dropped off before the loco pulled the train free of the platform.

He pictured Faulkner's cosy chat with their cadet. "We don't call this Scotland Yarder 'governor'. Likely's our governor. This man gets no better than 'boss.' The governor gets his tea and coffee first, he keeps his own chair and keep your eyes peeled for any wink from the governor that he wants to speak with us alone." (Storey's woolgathering had it word for word.)

At ten minutes past seven, when Storey's train weaved its way through Clapham Junction, the Chief Constable resigned and his office was sealed. A promising superintendent was already travelling from Liverpool and, although everyone knew that his appointment was temporary, he had resolved to conduct his evening meeting with his senior staff with all the discipline that the situation required. Storey, alone and asleep in his railway carriage, had been told enough to expect both moves. He prayed that the new regime would tolerate Skelton for longer than they should; the man needed room to make his mistakes.

Ask him, and he would have said that he'd dozed for no more than a few minutes but, when he came to and released the window blind, it was twilight and the train was pulling into a wayside station and he realised he'd gone through Woking and Basingstoke without knowing.

He walked into the corridor, pulled a leather strap that released a window and stepped back to avoid the smut from the engine. Further along the platform, a family was waiting for their pram to be lifted down from the guards van. Storey added another forty minutes to the schedule and guessed that he wouldn't be home before ten. He lit up, the train gathered speed and they were soon racing through the woods and heath of Hampshire army land.

Who killed Edie Winterton, his Snowflake girl? Skelton? Unlikely. Skelton was crooked, a dodgy dealer, but didn't have the look of a killer. Williams, Jean Paul and Dusty Ainsworth were outside bets with Forsyte and Miss Langworthy out in front. Yesterday he would have put his half crown on the dead Dominic Worth and nothing in Storey's water prompted him to move his money. But, as the train pulled into his station, a more disturbing thought wouldn't be pushed from the inspector's mind. Young Constable Harry had been at the scene, unsupervised and vulnerable.

His platform was deserted. He walked through the unmanned barrier and through the booking hall where a wireless was playing behind closed doors. He half expected Faulkner to be waiting with a car but he wasn't bothered when the sergeant wasn't there.

He pulled up his coat collar and stepped into the city at night.

Chapter Sixteen

The High Street was busy. Outside the Station Hotel, the motorcycle club was assembling for its all night ride through the forest. The licensee had sent a barmaid to stop them drinking on the pavements. She put up with some teasing, threatening to call the inspector from the other side of the road if she had any more trouble. Most of them were old soldiers with their best motorcycling days behind them. Even their talk of engines and gears wasn't as animated these days; their judgements could be delivered with a grunt or a shake of their heads.

"Hello, Likely!" called the biggest of them. "Got 'em on the run, have you?"

He slowed. His copper's instinct told him that the call had been an invitation to chat and a good copper never walked on from that. But he had an appointment with the man from the Yard. He looked across for any face that he recognised. Old Foster was there - Foster, who'd got a mention at Third Ypres and kept to the back of any crowd - and fat Mrs Crawley, built like a farm horse, who had taken her husband's place in the group when T.B. carried him off two years ago.

Storey excused himself with, "I'll be in the caff later on." They'd be on the road by then, they shouted.

Further up, a couple were leaning together on the tiled steps of the picture house. He wanted to kiss but the girl, no more than seventeen and looking very small, was having none of it. "Are you saying I'm not worth waiting for, Tom Daley? We won't be going in at all if you're not promising to behave." She wanted to know why he hadn't bought her a box of candies.

Storey crossed the main road at the fountain. The gutters were littered with debris from the street market. The road-sweeper had given up and was leaning on his broom while he waited for a water-cart. He took his pipe from his mouth and said, "We've a needie behind the Grayling, gov. You going to call up and have him brought in?" as Storey walked past. The bowl of the workman's pipe had been burnt out of shape and the stem was discoloured from years in the same mouth.

"I'll send someone, Sandy. Thanks for that."

He was making his way up the hill when he heard some lads playing football with a tin can in an alley. He felt an urge to join in, and twenty years ago, when he was a young copper patrolling this part of town through the night, he would have done so. Then he heard a woman scream from the same place.

He ran to the crown of the alley. Just a few yards down, it was as black as the inside of a barrel. He shouted, but the lads had moved on. He thought he could hear the girl sobbing, but that was water spilling out of a drainpipe. He'd no torch but he needed to investigate. He took half a dozen steps, uneasy that he could no longer be seen from the road. Hairs twitched on the back of his neck. He was thinking that he'd do better looking down from the rooftop when a heavy blow to his shoulders dropped him to his knees.

He tried to turn but the steel cap of a navvy's boot was going at his ribs, again and again like a power pump. He tried to make sense of it - one man, six foot, black clothing, wooden club - but looking up for more than a second left his face exposed and the punch came in like the bolt from a slaughterman's destroyer. His head swam, his eyes wouldn't work in one direction, he rolled over and spewed. He saw the club in the air, moved his head so that it caught his neck and then he tasted blood in his mouth. It would have snapped his collarbone if he hadn't hunched at the last instant. He wrapped his arms across his face and the man went in for a final kicking. He rolled over and tried to bury himself in the dirty brick wall. Christ, he thought, I'm going to choke in my own blood.

Then two hands grabbed the top of his coat and hauled him up. "You're through it, governor. He's buggered off." As he regained his focus, Sergeant Miller's face emerged from the darkness. "Go steady, boss. Don't try to move." The back of his glove was trying to clear the soddened face. "You're at the back of the Grayling. Christ almighty, your face has gone west. Don't talk." He repeated, "You're at the back of the Grayling. We'll get you into the lobby."

Waterman, the worst of Miller's friends, was called out to carry Storey's body through the pub's filthy kitchen. He did it like he was hauling a sack of King Edwards. He unfurled him at the bottom of some stairs where Drew Evans was waiting to clean him up. Drew Evans had been caught playing doctors at a renegade boxing match, two months before, and only God and the unworthies knew why he hadn't been charged.

"So how many struck off quacks have straightened you up, Likely? There's a first time for everything, eh?"

His shirt was off, his trousers undone and Evans was trying to get inside his ear while the Grayling's landlady washed his face from a saucepan of cold water. Storey looked down and the water was red, like weak tomato soup.

Evans caught what he was thinking. "It looks worse than it is," he promised. "Did he knock you out?"

Storey moaned; he couldn't talk and he wasn't going to try a shake of his head.

"So you knew what was going on, all through? Just talk with your eyes, that's the way to do it."

Storey made another noise.

Waterman was towering over their backs. "We've had our eye on you for some time, Likely. It's time you came unstuck but nothing like this. It's beneath human."

"I don't want him on show like this," the landlady decided. "Carry him up to the first floor front, boys, and someone get hold of his wife."

Chief Inspector Maynard Trump of the Metropolitan Police, D Division, kept out of conversation as he stood at the public bar and, before introducing himself to Storey, learned that men of the Grayling resented not that one of their policemen had been attacked but that a stranger had the gall to encroach on their territory to do it. Miller had made himself scarce but Waterman was there, repeating his doctrine that Likely Storey had been riding for a fall but the kicking in the alley had been more than was called for.

One man with a Fascist Union flash pinned to his lapel tapped his knuckle on the counter. "Look, you've got to understand. The thing about old Likely..."

"I've always liked him myself," countered a dwarf with a cloth cap and a walking stick. "He's good with old people."

"That's as maybe, Lofty, but he hates policemen. That's the thing about Storey. He says most of them don't know their jobs and those who do are too lazy to do it."

"Hates toffs too," said the midget.

"Oh, he can't stand toffs. You might say that he's no time for no one who's got on in life. Bitter."

"Very bitter."

This was too much of an opportunity to slip past Waterman.

"What did you say?"

"I said, bitter."

"Don't mind if I do," the big man answered and looked around to check who wasn't laughing at his joke. He leaned over the bar and called the landlady. "I don't like people playing darts when we're talking, Millie," he said quietly. "It's disrespectful."

She nodded and screwed a tea towel into a dirty glass.

Trump backed away. He carried his beer into the lobby and, unnoticed, walked up the stairs. He found Storey dressed,

136

bruised and smoothing his hair in front of a dressing table mirror.

He sat on a corner of the mattress. "I've suspended Skelton," he announced, "and told Debbie she's not to leave the office. The Merseyside Super has asked your Head to take over the Coldwater enquiry which means we've got both jobs."

Storey was trying to dab his lip into a more ordinary position. "A clever move. The county's got rot from the top to the bottom but the super from Merseyside's still got some good men there, if he can sort them out."

"I'm Mannie Trump of the Yard. Can you shake hands?"

Why did they always have to say 'of the Yard'? He countered, "I'm Storey of the Borough." He sensed that a cocked eyebrow would be painful. "Have you heard of me? I have worked with some of the best detectives in England."

"Derry Hampton mentioned you to my superintendent. Briefly."

"Yes, the Fahrenheit affair. An interesting case that was only resolved when Hampton played his hunch the Laura Tee was too much of a lady to select two pairs of knickers which were exactly the same. Did he tell you that? Your super?"

"I was worried that you might find it difficult to talk."

"I'm improving. Your company must be good for me."

"I know you don't need my help, Likely. That docket was some of the best detective work I've seen."

"Thank you, sir. Sergeant Faulkner is a good evidence officer."

"Janine is waiting at the station but I wanted a word with you before I take you up there." He spoke as if Storey needed a wheelchair. "What do you make of this ambush? Are you closer to the killer than you think?"

"I'm sure of it. It was too heavy handed to be revenge from the boys at county." Storey sighed heavily. "But I can't make much sense of it. We need Faulkner to get the rest of Forsyte's story. He's our best lead so far."

"He wanted to resign from the Watch Committee but your H.C. talked him out of it. There's too much politics in this, Storey. It's dogging our thinking." He stood up. "Talk in the pub suggests you were ambushed by an unknown outsider. And those people down there would have known if it had been a local job."

Storey agreed. "They're about the worst we've got." He turned away from the mirror. "How do I look?"

"Grim. But she wants to play nursemaid so I guess you'll do fine."

Janine let him sleep in until ten the next morning. After breakfast, she sat him at her dressing table and worked on his face for twenty minutes. Storey said that she might have been playing with one of her old dolls. By the time he got to the office, Faulkner was out on enquiries, Trump was in conference with the Head and Debbie was rearranging the outer office. "H.C. has given the accountant's office to the new man," she said. The place felt warmer than it had done for months and she'd gone as far as scouring the gas ring. "You look a bit swollen, chief."

He gave a hum with no meaning. "I'd like some toast. I've had breakfast, could eat a horse but will make do with toast." He disappeared into his den but left the door open,

He unpackaged a new pipe which had arrived in the morning post. Whenever he bought a new pipe, he promised that it was for looking at only; he had his family of old pipes to smoke and wouldn't risk introducing an unknown cousin. But this unpretentious offering, straight stemmed and simply made from pear-wood by a fifth generation tobacconist in Ringwood, won him over. He would smoke it, but only until the bruises healed on his face. As he savoured the sweetness of a first smoke, he got used to being in familiar surroundings again. On the second bowlful, he sat motionless and waited for Cadet Holden.

She knocked, made room on a corner on his crowded desk for the toast, marmalade and coffee and said she was halfway through putting things in date order. "Sergeant Faulkner doesn't want them A-Z. He says he can usually remember when but rarely the names." (They both knew that Faulkner had explained the working of Storey's memory, not his own.) "I'll get on."

But he didn't nod, or say yes, or dismiss her in any way. He waited for as long as half a minute - it felt like more. Then he took the pipe just half an inch from his mouth and asked, "What went on between you and Julie from the Red Rose?"

She felt her throat blush. He hadn't suggested that she should sit down and she was standing on the rug in the middle of the room.

"I read your statement a dozen times on the train. Do you know what I think? I think you ended up not liking each other. It went well to begin with but then you stopped asking questions and just listened to what she told you. You fell out, didn't you?"

"I don't know what you mean, chief."

He paused, looked at the clock and said, "We've an hour before Sergeant Faulkner gets back. Perhaps it's fair that he asks the questions and not me?"

"No. It's nothing, chief."

She stepped backwards and perched on the very edge of the easy chair. Storey gave the slightest shake of his head, saying nothing, and she stood up again. Inch by inch, she came back to the patch of rug in front of his desk.

"You're very nervous," he said with feigned naivety. "Let me tell you something."

She nodded.

"When you don't know what to do with your hands, put them behind your back and hold on tight." He put his pipe in his mouth and pushed the chair back from the desk. "This is serious, you know? You've made a statement that might be placed before the court. It's not likely, but you could be cross examined by learned counsel. I don't want anyone from this office to go into the witness box without all the answers in their head."

She coughed to clear her throat. "She tried to kiss me, chief, but I would let her and I don't want you to do anything about it."

"Why would I?"

"I feel sorry for her."

"Yes. Your statement read like someone who feels sorry." He picked up a slice of toast, checked both sides and said, "It's not the same as when it's done on a fire."

Faulkner marched into the suite, hung his cap behind the outer door and, with a passing, "Morning, cadet!" (though he couldn't see the girl) went straight to Storey. "Do you want Skelton kippered or fried?" He acknowledged Deborah with a fleeting nod.

"I wouldn't bother to chose, as long as he's drawn and quartered."

Faulkner looked at the bruises and winced. "Ouch, that's grim."

"You've been to see Red Rose Julie?"

He nodded. "I thought she might have some more to tell us."

Storey came in quickly. "As far as I'm concerned, she tried to kiss our cadet and our cadet resisted."

"Of course, governor," he said smartly. "But she also told me that your favourite restaurateur, Williams, spent yesterday trying to track down French Jasper."

Storey's mouth opened but nothing came out for a few seconds. "Of course, the boots. And that's why he didn't say anything. Thank god, he didn't use one of this motorcycle chains on me."

"And Jasper has been Skelton's grass since Adam was a lad."

"It's not evidence."

"Not yet, but it will be." He bent towards the fire and warmed his hands. "This place has warmed up since our Debbie's been confined to barracks. How are you getting on, girl?"

Storey's phone rang. The others watched his face drop as he listened.

"Grab your hat, sergeant. " He banged his thigh as he rushed around the desk. "Dusty Ainsworth is outside Forsyte's place and he won't answer the door."

Chapter Seventeen

"This is my fault, governor," Faulkner said as he held the car, straining on its leash, at Market Street traffic lights. "Midday, and the bloody fruit van turns up to deliver produce in the middle of town. Jammed. Look over your shoulder. No one's moving as far back as Boots."

Likely looked idly at people passing by on the pavement. "What we need is a policeman," he muttered. It was never funny, he knew that, and it wasn't now.

Faulkner squeezed the steering wheel. "It's my damned fault. I should have called on him this morning rather than Red Rose Julie."

The lights changed to green but the traffic wouldn't allow him to move forward. Three cars behind, someone started blowing their horn

"Why did you?" Storey asked, and leaned back so that he could bring his pipe and matches from his coat pocket.

"The same reason as you're thinking, governor. I wanted to protect Debbie. Her story obviously had more to it."

Storey laid down the line. "The girl tried to kiss her and Deborah resisted."

Enough said.

"He was our best lead," Faulkner insisted, still cross with himself. "Sixty-seven minutes, I had him in your office and he never denied murder."

They moved, a length and a half. When the fruit van tried to turn in the road, Faulkner lost patience. Shouting and waving his hat in the air, he strode from the car, its door left wide open, and, with coat tails flapping around him broke all the rules of point duty. He threatened the van driver with the chopping board if he moved another inch. He cleared both pavements of pedestrians and ordered the opposing lines of traffic to drive through on both paths, making an island of the van. When the traffic was flowing well, he stopped everything and gave the van driver a count of fifteen to get out of his sight.

"That's how 'Beaker' Claythorne taught us to do it," he said before Storey had chance to comment. He did battle with the gear box. "Which doesn't make it any less my fault." The car swayed on its chassis as he turned towards the old estates.

Dusty Ainsworth's antics over Forsyte's front flowerbeds had provoked his neighbours to call the uniform brigade. Two had arrived on bicycles while the local patrol arrived on foot and unhurried. Across the street, Peggy Patterson saw it all from her round window, half way up the stairs. She telephoned her husband, a sergeant at county headquarters - who, by listening on one instrument and speaking into another, transmitted the running commentary to his equivalence at Willow Place.

"We've had to break in the french windows at the back," said a young constable on the side path. Another, squatting beside the ornamental pond so that he could observe the fishes, straightened up and said, "He's shot himself, governor. He's laid out on the other side of those glass doors."

"Then stay on your bloody feet, man," he barked.

He muttered, "Get his collar number, Faulkner," as he pressed against the cast iron door handle.

Harrison-Potter had already completed his 'once over' the body and was seated at the dead man's sideboard drawing pictures in a pocket book. "Tell me, how are the best detectives in England? Three deaths, inspector, and you're no nearer solving the puzzle."

It was a small dining room, laid out for a man who liked to look out on this garden as he ate his breakfast alone. Just one small table and the sideboard. Two chairs without arms. A clock, ten minutes fast. No photographs. (Storey was always quick to notice that.)

Captain Forsyte had fallen into a corner. He was properly shaved and dressed, like most suicides. "Best sports jacket and golfing trousers and shoes laced tightly," he observed. "When they undress him, they'll find fresh underwear, probably pressed to a crease." Forsyte had managed to stretch his legs and roll on his side so that his back was towards the window. No one looking in could have got a good view of what he had done to himself. Storey reflected that this was the death of a man who had wanted to behave decently to the last.

"You got here very quickly?" he grumbled.

"We do our best, inspector." Dr Harrison-Potter placed his pencil in the hinge of the notebook. "Considerate, don't you think, to take a shot through the heart? No one has to clean half his brains from the carpet. Give them a month and they'll have this old rug in an auction. Head jobs are always so messy." He followed their survey of the scene and repeated, "Three deaths, Likely; they'll be after your hide before long."

"Scotland Yard have the case now. They'll sort it before lunchtime, I'm sure."

Faulkner was kneeling beside the corpse.

"The gun had been pressed to his heart." the doctor told him. "From inside his very best shirt, I think. He's lying in a pool of blood but his clothing took most of it. A very clean way of doing it."

"Thankfully, there's little to detect in these circumstances," Faulkner said quietly, as much to himself as the others.

"We are not surprised that Forsyte killed himself," Storey reported. "We know the background. Even so, we are somewhat sorry that we didn't manage to speak with him again, before he decided to shoot himself. Did he live here alone?"

"If I see a policeman, I'll ask him."

Outside, a uniformed copper was beckoning Faulkner. Storey deliberately turned a blind eye, provoking the constable to wave with both hands and go up and down on his heels. "Bloody clown. You better deal with him, sergeant."

Without a word, Faulkner stepped through the french windows, leaving the inspector alone with the doctor.

"You know, doctor," Storey sighed patiently, "I try to like you but it's always difficult to find a reason."

"I'm sorry." The doctor slipped the book inside his jacket. "Yes, the captain lived on his own. He and his wife parted a dozen years ago. He lived a rather pitiful life. He never found his land fit for heroes. Scotland Yard, you say? Well, who's ever in charge will need to tear up their lists of suspects, inspector. With this one, they start again."

Storey felt that he was three fences behind the field. "Are you saying this is not a suicide?"

"Impossible." The doctor was a bald headed man with red patches on his cheeks that seemed to push them forward. He had doctors' fingers - long, probing, white from too much scrubbing, with palpy looking nails trimmed back. He wore only three piece Montague suits with faint stripes in the thread and, every evening, spent time bulling the tips of his black shoes. "What can I tell you? His murderer had never met him before and was rather a clown." He allowed the detective a few moments to catch up with his deduction, then revealed, "The gun has been laid at his left hand. Forsyte was right handed but while it's not usual for a right handed man to shoot with his left, that would be impossible in this case."

Storey turned away to look again at the body but he couldn't follow the doctor's reasoning.

"Forsyte always kept that hand gloved. As a young subaltern, he impaled himself on the barbed wire of the Somme. The tendons were ripped apart and the palms twisted where the medics strapped it up for the wound to heal. I'm not criticising; they could do little else in the circumstances. Battle injuries are always difficult. They patched him up and moved on to the next poor sod. They probably didn't expect him to live beyond a few days. He's also got a hideous scar between his shoulders and down the length of his back. I have always thought that he visited his bullying mistress because he hated his body. He wanted it punished. But let's not theorise about that. Inspector Storey, this man had no feeling in his left hand and certainly couldn't move his fingers. Clearly, you're looking for a killer who didn't know he was lame. A stranger. The bleeding stopped only a few minutes before I got here. He was killed no more than forty minutes ago."

"Sergeant Faulkner!"

Faulkner poked his head through the doors. "A witness is asking to speak with you, governor. I've told her to wait in the garden."

The whole thing irritated. He had been outsmarted by the killer, the doctor had been quick to pick up on it and the police were drawing a slow third place. He clenched his fists in his pockets and stiffened his shoulders. He said in a rigid voice, "Trump of the Yard is required at the scene. He has a hot murder on his hands. Find a sergeant and organise an immediate house to house. I want every soul in this street questioned. Someone must have seen the succession of callers."

The witness was a woman with a gaunt figure and a face that was full of no sleep. In her forties, Storey guessed badly. Her simple cotton dress had been long out of fashion and had no idea how it was supposed to sit on her skinny frame. "You're going to be cross with me, inspector," she warned.

"I don't think so. I think you're the one person who'll cheer me up." He saw that his favourite constable was close enough to take it all in. He sent him to find two chairs. "We'll sit and watch the fishes, shall we?"

"I live in the Denning Flats. I was Edie's next door neighbour. She said I wasn't getting involved in anything but three people have been killed and I can't see how I'm not in trouble. You're going to charge me with something, aren't you?"

"You're going too fast, Miss -- ?"

"Sandy. Don't you remember me, inspector?"

"Miss Sandy, start at the beginning."

"No, just Sandy. Sandy Avory. Mrs Avory by rights, not Miss anything, but I like people to call me Sandy. It stops explanations."

When the P.C. came out with two chairs from the kitchen, Storey said, "If someone can have a word with next door, we might have two teas. Ask for a couple of biscuits, constable. These are difficult times. Now Sandy, from the start of it all, but please go slowly. Everyone's ahead of me this morning."

She wobbled as she balanced the chair on the uneven ground. "Edie said that she was going to play a joke on you. She knew that I didn't like you and she said I could join in. It would be like getting my own back, she said. And when she told me, it sounded a wonderful idea. Everyone would end up laughing at you."

"Why don't you like me?"

She said, as if it was obvious and a waste of her breath, "Because you wanted to arrest me when I was in my dressing gown. In 1933, inspector, when I was a nipper. Nineteen, that's all I was, and living on my own. Derek Smart had walked out on me and the baby and you said I'd done a burglary."

"Of course, you're Sandra Smart. I never did get you for it, did I?"

"I'm Mrs Avory now. At least Hubert married me before he found better options which is more than that Derek Smart ever did. The woman at the station said you should never have arrested me in my nightclothes. She said it was despicable."

"So you thought it would be great fun to help Edie with her prank."

"I had to pretend that I lived in number 239 and if anyone came to the door I had to say that no one called Edith had ever lived there or thereabouts. That was part of the joke, you see, that you'd believed a story from someone who never existed."

The constable delivered tea and biscuits on a tin tray from Coronation Day. The neighbour leaned over the fence and Storey waved a thank you. She didn't move, even when she realised that she was too far away to listen.

"But someone killed poor Edie," he said.

"And I felt dreadful about it. I asked all the questions. I even went to the back of the Red Rose and told him that I wouldn't shift until he told me who'd done it. I was thinking, the best way of getting out of trouble was to find out what happened."

"But he wouldn't tell you."

"Mr Storey, Bert Williams knows nothing about it. He's like a scaredy cat. He says if you don't get the killer quick, Bert Williams will be next."

"Well, you tell him that Mr Storey is trying his best."

She collected her handbag from between her feet and produced a clutch of photographs.

"I found these in Edie's flat. I took them because I knew that Edie wouldn't want anyone else to have them. But now, Mr Worth has been killed and Captain Forsyte this morning and I thought if I don't do something with them, I'm going to be in awful trouble."

Behind the french windows, Trump of the Yard was directing an officer with a tape measure and making mincemeat of Dr Harrison-Potter Sergeant Horndean, who had turned up to retrieve the pool car only to be put in charge of the house to house enquiries, was standing to attention as he delivered his first report from his pocket book. Faulkner had taken Dusty Ainsworth next door, insisting that the woman of the house should stay at the back garden fence until he had finished interviewing his suspect.

Likely Storey was eating one biscuit with the next wedged between his little finger and the fat of his hand. "These are naughty pictures, Sandra," he said before tucking them into the top of his waistcoat and reaching for his cup and saucer.

"Would you like some more?"

"You've got some?"

"Tea's what I meant." She turned and called to the woman at the fence. When that didn't work, she got up from her chair and walked over. Storey pocketed the last of the biscuits.

In the first picture, Edie was lying between Dorothy Langworthy's legs and squeezing the woman's breast so that the cameraman had a good view of it. Neither had any clothes on and Edie was trying to get her legs to part without disrupting the pose.

"She says she needs her empties first," Sandra reported and left Storey to leaf through the photographs as she collected the crockery and returned the tray.

Every picture seemed worse than the previous and there was nothing tempting about them. The director had wanted the most explicit show possible, nothing less. 'They're all going to gaol,' Storey thought. The models, the photographer and processor, and anyone who had sold the copies. Then he wondered how many of them were already beyond the law.

"How much trouble am I in?" Sandra asked.

"Did you know about them before? Have you got any others? Have you sold any or given any away?"

"Not at all, Inspector Storey. Honest, I knew nothing about them and I'm scared to death. Three people have been killed and Bertie Williams says they won't be the last."

"If you're telling me the truth and if you keep telling the truth, you're not in any trouble." He took a notebook from his pocket and wrote a receipt in careful handwriting. Sandra signed the reverse. "Did you bring them in a bag?"

She pulled one from her handbag. Storey wrapped them up and put them away. "Our second round of tea's here," he said, nodding towards the fence.

This time, there was a plate of lightly spread jam sandwiches on the tray, and left-over pickings of roast chicken in a sugar bowl.

"When the old woman went in to make the tea, I heard her confiding to your sergeant. She said that Jean Paul had been with the captain earlier on. You've heard of Jean Paul?"

Chapter Eighteen

"This is exceedingly pleasant Mr Williams. My sergeant was just saying that if ever our enquiries bring us to this part of the town, we must drop in for one of your cream teas."

Williams was saying nothing. He was working the cafe on his own. Taking orders and making them up, not to mention the cooking and cleaning. If the police thought they could hound him, well, this time he'd stand up for himself.

It was half past four and the Red Rose restaurant should have been busier. The pavements were crowded with local schoolchildren, queuing for buses, standing outside shops and hanging around the street corners. Some were collecting car numbers at the crossroads while others swapped cigarette cards. The most rowdy waved soccer scarves which they had dared not bring out at school for fear of confiscation. It was a commotion which usually sent grown-ups into places like the Red Rose, yet there were only two other customers - a couple who had been married longer than Storey had been in the borough police and enjoyed their paste sandwiches slowly. With every sip of tea, they whispered what a good strength it had.

"I'm keeping out of the way," Storey explained to his sergeant. "Trump of the Yard is well on with the case. But I remember old Evanshaw; he always kept a distance when he needed to tie up the loose ends, and I'll tell you, sergeant, the itch tells me that I've never been closer to finishing a case. How many detectives has Trump brought in? Sergeant, we are going to get there before him."

"He's like a steam hammer, governor." Faulkner countered, idly stirring his tea. "He's turned Jean Paul's place upside down. The bookshop was only a front. The backroom was set out like a studio, with a darkroom upstairs and enough old prints and negs to fill a Pickford's truck of tea-chests."

"The bookshop was a front?" Storey laughed. "The Watch Committee won't like Trump saying that. Our Scotland Yarder had better get a grip of the politics. Jean Paul has restocked their select every month for two years. That's how he knew Skelton's secret passage into the nick. He'd been using the canteen waste chute to haul the library stock up and down."

Faulkner laid the spoon in his saucer. "We've got him, governor."

Storey shook his head. "Not yet. Oh, he'll go to gaol for licentious publication but I don't want him in gaol. I want him to take the drop for three murders. When we've finished with the Red Rose, get back to the office and make sure Trump doesn't hold onto Jean Paul. I want him free for another thirty-six hours. Play the role of an evidence officer and Trump will listen to you. He respects you for that. And warn him off the politics of the affair. That'll scare him out of his boots."

He raised a hand and called loudly for Williams. "I'm surprised that you're not busier!"

"I've put the closed sign up, Mr Storey." He was drying his hands on a towel when he reached them and trying to keep everyone's voice down. "You saw me do that as soon as you walked in."

"But it's not five o'clock yet."

"Please, be reasonable, Mr Storey. I can't throw these people out. Surely, you can wait until the place is empty."

"Mr Williams, we can wait until the sun goes down" he bawled. "Tell me, does the sun ever set on the Red Rose cafe. To me, it's always seemed like a house that never closes."

He laid his dry pipe on the table and, when his hand went to his jacket, they thought that he was seeking his tobacco pouch.

Instead, he produced Sandra's brown paper package. He looked around, raised his eyebrows and spread the pictures before them.

"Ah no, for Christ's sake, Storey! Who are you! Look, I've got customers!"

Williams backed away from the table and busied himself with the old couple. "You don't understand. I must chase you away. People are having babies here and I need to contact the council. It didn't ought to be allowed. This is a nice part of town." He had collected their cups, saucers and plates, and was helping them out of their chairs. "These two gentlemen are hooligans. I think they are demanding money. It's better you are out of the place. Please, you come again soon."

Storey stood up so that he could bow gently as the couple left.

"Inspector, you're hounding me. I never had nothing to do with those pictures." He was walking around the room with his arms in the air, beseeching first one wall then another. "Sandra was the first to show them to me and I told her: take them to Mr Storey. You ask her. She'll tell you what I said."

"She says you're a scaredy cat. I can see why." Storey curled a finger to direct him to their table. "Now, be quiet, Williams. There is something interesting that I want to show you. I think, we need to look at it together." He pushed one of the prints forward. "Do you own a magnifying glass? It can be quite difficult to spot in a poor light, but if you look carefully, you see, through the window, there is just the shape of your old motorcycle. Now that's interesting, don't you think?"

"It's my back room. Of course, it is. I won't deny that. I let people use it"

Storey took his time. He charged and lit his pipe and was leaning back as he puffed, when he asked, "Lovers?"

Williams was nodding but hesitated before confirming, "If you like, lovers."

"Like Dorothy Langworthy and Edie Winterton? Lovers like that?"

"Oh, what do you call these women? Are they lovers? Yes, all right, I agree. Langworthy and Winterton. Lovers." He started to jab his finger at the policemen. "But, you listen. Both of you listen. Mr Faulkner, you write down what I say. I didn't know Jean Paul was taking pictures. For god's sake, ask him. He'll tell you I punched him on the nose. I shouted at him. I yelled, who's going to use the Red Rose if they think we're taking pictures."

Storey took his pipe from his mouth and queried the underside as if there were some sort of design fault. "How much?"

"A fair rent, Mr Storey."

"A fair rent for a lover's hidey-hole? I see." He stuck out his bottom lip. "What would you say, Sergeant Faulkner? What's a fair rent? You see, Williams, when I put you in front of the magistrates for keeping a disorderly house ..."

"Ah, no." He slapped his arms to his side and went round in circles. "There you are! Hounding me again."

"So it wasn't a disorderly house? It was just two friends. Langworthy and Winterton and not one other soul?"

"Yes. Just that. No one else."

Williams fell silent and sat at one of the empty tables. He wiped his eyes. "It is difficult," he moaned. "Only, I want to do what is right. Only, doing what is right is not always the same as saying what is right. It's saying and doing. It's tying me in knots."

Faulkner left his governor's table and joined Williams. He crouched forward, so that Williams had to crouch too before he could listen. "It's the governor, Bertie," mumbled the sergeant. "He hasn't eaten, hasn't slept for days. I can see it in his eyes; he wants to care for you, Bertie, like we all do. But I can see in his eyes, he's losing patience with you. I'm worried, Bertie, what might happen if he gets cross. You do remember my governor when he's cross?"

"Then perhaps you should tell him, Mr Faulkner, that there was also Worth's wife."

"Worth's wife? Some sort of shop is that?"

"Mrs Margot Worth. She was a treacherous woman, Mr Faulkner. I could tell you stories about her that would keep us busy for hours. The intrigues. The money grabbing. He should never have married her. You ask, many people say that."

"I see. Mr and Mrs Worth used to hire your back room?"

"No, you're not listening to me. Mrs Worth wanted to spend time with Miss Langworthy."

"Dorothy too?"

"Yes, as well as Edie."

"Three of them?"

"No. Not together. Mrs Worth wanted to but Edie wouldn't."

"So who did Edie want?"

"Miss Langworthy."

"But not Mrs Worth."

"I said that. Mrs Worth wanted Miss Langworthy too."

"Williams, I'm not sure I can keep up with this. Go slowly for me." He licked the lead of his pencil and turned the page of his pocketbook. "Now, going through them, one at a time."

Storey had left the restaurant and was smoking his pipe beneath the little porch.

"You mustn't let him take me to court, Mr Faulkner. My pretty cafe would be ruined."

Faulkner kept his head down. "And your brothel."

"No!" William's shot away from the table. "Why do they say these horrible things about me?" He was addressing the walls again. "I am telling them all that I know!"

"Was Worth blackmailing you? He found out the truth about the Red Rose and you murdered him."

"No! I was here. I have tickets to prove that I was in the Red Rose." He stood still and tried to work out what the sergeant was thinking.

"Come and sit down, Williams."

He shook his head. "He never asked for money," he said quietly. "I'll not put the blame on a dead man. It was Jean Paul who offered him money to keep him quiet."

"Where were you between midnight and six on Sunday morning?"

"When Edith was killed? Christ, sergeant, you can't think I did that. Not to poor Edie. I was here." Then a clever smile brightened his withered face. "No, no I wasn't. I was with the motorcycle club. The president split us into two groups. Your inspector saw them getting ready on Wednesday night." He was nodding excitedly. "That's right. One group did the all night ride on Wednesday, but the president asked my group to go ahead on Sunday morning."

"And this morning? Where were you when Captain Forsyte was shot?"

"I went to see Sandra, but she wasn't in. The traders on the market will tell you, I was hanging around for hours."

"Come and sit down, Williams. I want us to talk, one to the other. You have pictures of Mrs Worth and Miss Langworthy?"

"You want to see Margot Worth with no clothes on?" Williams asked.

Faulkner put his head lower, only inches from the table top, drawing Williams closer. "Williams, you are a disgusting reptile," he said moderately. "No, I don't want to see Mrs Worth undressing. I want to know if Jean Paul took pictures of her."

He nodded, just once. "Worth paid him. He wanted the evidence; she was a bad woman to her husband, this Margot Worth."

Chapter Nineteen

Gershwin's rhapsody was drawing to its close but, because Janine was dozing in his lap, Storey couldn't reach across to lift the needle from the record. He counted fifty three clicks, each one a revolution, before the gramophone wound down and the needle came to rest.

"We ought to try that little place in Orchard Street one evening," she said sleepily, without opening her eyes. She pressed her elbow into the side of his stomach, making herself comfy.

"It's a silly thing to say."

She pushed harder with the elbow, drawing back and looking at his face. "Silly?"

"Yes. The needle comes to rest. It's doesn't. The turntable goes round and round while the needle stays in one place, so it can't come to rest."

She dropped her head against his chest and closed her eyes. After a few moments silence, she suggested quietly. "It starts on the outside of the record and comes to rest near the centre. See, it does move."

"Margaret Horndean told you about Orchard Street. I saw them in there on Wednesday evening, on my way up from the station." He closed his eyes. It was half past ten and he meant to be in bed before eleven. Their supper had been cleared away, Janine had made their last beakers of Horlicks and the evening, like the gramophone, was winding down.

"It's got a man who plays the fiddle while you eat," she said.

"Nine o'clock tomorrow night, then. I'll reserve their best table and you can wear that frock."

She sniggered. "The one with the pretty underwear underneath?"

"And those pretty stockings that go nicely with the white at the tops of your legs."

"You want me to show the white at the top of my legs," she teased, inviting him to contradict her.

"No need. You wear the stockings and I'll picture the tops."

She sat up, pressing her knees on his legs, and stretched to wind the gramophone and return the needle to the beginning of the tune.

"It's like sitting with some ungainly great dane on my knees."

"You're a scurrilous old elephant," she said, as she resettled her little body. "I hope you know that."

"I promise I'll be home early. I need to interview Miss Langworthy before breakfast, then I'll have the case wrapped up before lunchtime. Faulkner will want to work late on the file but the inspector will come home to his wife, early."

She stifled a yawn. "Is my husband one of England's great detectives?"

It was question that deserved a serious answer. With his eyes still closed and flexing his nose to get rid of an itch, he told her no. "I have neither Evanshaw's intuition nor Arthur Dowding's order of thought. Dodridge was good and maybe I'm better, but Dodridge's excitement was infectious. I don't excite, Janine. I can't be a great detective in England because I don't like many people there. Hampton's Fahrenheit Case was wonderful to watch; it had so many threads."

"You do."

"Do what?"

"You do excite Janine."

"I wouldn't be the same detective without her," he admitted.

The record was reaching her favourite passage. "I've never understood why they call it the Fahrenheit case."

158

The doorbell chimed.

"Because it boiled over at 212, Denning Placade. Someone wants to come in. We'll leave them. It's nearly eleven."

"They're knocking now. It sounds urgent, Likely."

While Janine answered the door, Storey collected the evening papers from the carpet and moved his smoking paraphernalia to an occasional table.

Deborah Holden tumbled into the room with her handbag open and her coat flying behind her. "I've found something important, chief!" She was waving one of the rude photographs.

Storey took his position on the hearth rug and showed her to the armchair. She collapsed into it. "Mr Trump told me to go through a crate of Jean Paul's pictures and look what I found. It's marvellous!"

"It's not," he said grimly, having pulled out a shirt tail to polish the bowl of his pipe. "It's not marvellous at all. He should never have given you such a job. God knows what your father would say."

But she was smug, delighted and close to delirious. "He'd say that I was one of the greatest detectives in the land!"

Storey grunted and collected the filthy picture that she was wafting around his sitting-room. "I shall telephone your father about this in the morning. I don't want him thinking it happened on my watch."

"Oh, don't be so... sorry, chief." Debbie put her fingertips to her lips and tried to look chastened.

The shot showed Dusty and Langworthy and Margot Worth together and Langworthy looked ugly, like a neglected nag from the forest. Thank the Lord, she had kept her knickers on while Dusty had found a chemise. But Margot Worth was naked, plump and pink. He immediately caught the picture's significant but didn't want to poach the girl's best moment.

"Explain. Why are you so chuffed, Cadet Holden?"

"Because the clock on the mantelpiece and the newspaper headline show that it was taken at Jean Paul's studio while Edith Winterton was being murdered in Coldwater Place. He'll use it as an alibi but it will do him no good. This evidence will hang him, won't it, chief?"

He passed it to Janine who responded cheerfully, "You wouldn't have a clue when she shops along High Street. The more you tell me about Margot Worth, the harder it is to believe. I mean, just look at the bulges. No woman can hide fat like that and not be scolded in church. Oh, I'd love to show the girls at the institute."

"I don't think that's the point," Storey said and snatched it back.

Debbie elaborated. "If you were taking naughty pictures ..."

"Which is unlikely."

"But you wouldn't - oh yes, I see. Un-Likely. Sorry, chief. The thing is, you wouldn't leave things in the frame that betray where it was taken. And the newspaper headline? Who wants to see a newspaper in a photo like that? It's a deliberate cheat, chief. They want us to think that they were in Jean Paul's studio at the time of the murder."

Storey nodded. "Instead, it shows us that they were all part of the cover up."

Chapter Twenty

Early morning on Coldwater Place, where the first murder had been committed less than two weeks before, was a damp and misty scene without people or colour. It had none of the promise of the town centre, where delivery vans were at work and folk had already set to their day's labour, where noise from windows and doors said that even if the late-comers had yet to take in the fresh air, they were near to it. At Coldwater Place a solitary cat crossed the road on her way home. Storey, standing at the telephone kiosk which had been Constable Harry's sentry box on the night of butchery, tried to transport himself back to the time when one furtive movement - a hurried look from a drawn curtain, the gingerly taken footsteps of a man on his heels or the last worried look over a woman's shoulder - could have been enough to alert the young policeman. If Storey had been keeping obs that night, he would have chosen one of the balconies overlooking the street. But P.C. Harry was no detective.

He pressed two-pence into the coin box and counted the rings before Miss Langworthy answered. For all her protestations, he could tell that she had been awake for some time. I'm a weary detective, he wanted to say, come to listen to your lies. "I thought a few moments warning was fair, Miss Langworthy. I'm about to knock on your door."

"It's not six o'clock, inspector."

"I thought you'd prefer to have it over and done with before your neighbours are about. I can wait."

But no, no, she said. "I shall have the door open for you. I've already spoken to the police."

"That was county, Miss Langworthy. Scotland Yard have the case now."

This woman, he decided, he disliked more than any of the others.

You weren't expecting Edith Winterton that night, he rehearsed as he made his way to Number 18. I want you to explain why she was calling on you. Did you telephone anyone as you saw her approach?

"Did Red Rose Julie spend that night with you," he asked when he was sitting in the threadbare easy chair. "I'd prefer to find out without asking the girl."

"Goodness me, is that what you call her?"

"Dreadful, isn't it? But policemen find themselves using their own shorthand in a case like this."

"And your nickname for me?"

"Just Langworthy. No more than that." Without getting close, he smelled the weak antiseptic on her breath and she'd emphasised the diseased yellow hue of her fingernails by polishing them to a gloss. "I should say, this won't be our only conversation today. After a few questions here, I shall ask you to prepare for a longer interview at Borough Police Station."

"Routine, is it?"

"Well, a little more than routine. I need to deal with some loose ends before I make my arrest."

"So you know who killed Edith and the others?"

He couldn't get rid of that image of Margot Worth kissing this woman's face with her tongue. He was sure that the tongue would have touched moss growing on the hidden side of her teeth.

He repeated, "Was Julie here all night?"

"She has never been to Coldwater Place, inspector. I think things may have been safer if she had accepted my invitations but they wouldn't have it."

"They?"

"The others."

"No, you must do better than that. You see, Jean Paul was very persistent. Even with Edith out of the way, he still pursued the girl. That's why she ran away from the cafe. Oh, she had stood up to his attempts to draw her into his web of disgusting depravity but the murder scared the girl out of her wits. So, who was against ruining the girl's life?"

"By implication, who was for it? Inspector, I think you are a very nasty piece of work. None of us are depraved. Our little indulgences have been in private and should have harmed no one. Yet, you judge everyone in terms of yes and no, for and against, with no room for wavering on either side. No one wanted to ruin Julie. That is the answer to your question but, of course, it's no good to you."

"I think Edith came here to persuade you to change your mind about the girl. I need to know who was on the girl's side and who thought Jean Paul's idea was a good one."

"So, it was Jean Paul's idea? Inspector, I think you are a long way from uncovering all those truths about us. But I will swear one thing to you. It was Mr Skelton's idea that you should be discouraged from making further enquiries. He had already been suspended from duty and, once you were put in charge of both murders, he feared that you might draw him into your investigation. He paid one of his cronies to attack you. Dusty was very angry with him. She called it stirring the pot. Do you believe me?"

He bowed his head. This woman had cleverly avoided his questions but he had gained sufficient information to proceed with the arrests. He invited her to tea in his office at half past ten that morning. "By all means, warn the others. The whole merry band will be there."

"Tell me. If you decide that I did not kill Edie..."

"Or Dominic Worth?"

"Or indeed, the captain. What will happen to me? Will I be charged for making love to Edie and Margot Worth?"

"Miss Langworthy, each one of you allowed herself to be photographed. You were part of Jean Paul's racket."

"But if we can show we knew nothing about that?"

"Surely, you must expect to be prosecuted."

She drew back from the argument. "It will be quite a scandal," she said as she showed him to her door before he was ready.

Chapter Twenty One

Detective Inspector Brian 'Likely' Storey of the Borough Police placed two photographs at the front of his desk and identified each character with the point of a pencil. "Mrs Worth and Miss Ainsworth. Miss Winterton and Miss Langworthy." He looked up. "And behind the camera, Mr Jean Paul, respected bookseller of this parish. A bookseller by appointment, no less. He replenishes our Watch Committee's library each month."

He opened his drawer, found a new box of Captain Webb matches and lit his pipe. He said, as he got it going, "The poor lady who walked through walls cannot be with us this morning. Together, we are going to explain why." The grey tobacco smoke drifted in front of his face.

"Where's Williams?" Jean Paul protested and leaned forward to stand up, but Sergeant Faulkner's hand was immediately on his shoulder. Jean Paul was proud and disgruntled and so, at this moment, the most impressive; not that Storey had time for any of them. When they had first taken their places, he'd thought, 'A bad lot.'

"You cannot allow him to walk free after all he's done," the bookseller insisted.

Storey held his pipe to one side. "Even Mr Williams is surprised by the strength of his alibis. My sergeant could set out the details for you. Williams did none of these killings and we needn't bother with him."

"But he will be prosecuted, won't he?" Miss Langworthy pressed. "Inspector, not one of us here is guilty of murder and,

165

if you've only the photographs to use against us, Williams must be caught in the net."

The four suspects were seated on a row of hard-backed chairs, each facing Storey's judgement and unable to easily draw support from one another. Dusty Ainsworth, the rough diamond of the group. Margot Worth, a cut above. And so, driven by a wickedness more ingrained? Storey wondered. Jean Paul, usually so composed and taciturn with a phony primness; now, his nerves were showing. And number four, the woman he disliked most of all, Miss Langworthy. Faulkner had warned him not to detest her.

Storey drew breath. "Ladies and gentlemen, of all the great detectives for whom I've worked, I have to say that Mr Evanshaw was the best. Without fail, this gentleman could tell us a murderer within forty eight hours of a case. It took him longer to assemble the evidence of course, but he had the intuition of a true master detective. One evening in the Pegasus, I asked him for the secret behind such cleverness. Miss Ainsworth, can you guess what he said?"

Dusty Ainsworth had taken a handkerchief from her handbag and was twisting it around her fingers. "I don't think I ever met him," she said. For the same reason, Margot Worth had opened a phial of scent and kept dabbing behind her ears.

"Motive. That's what Evanshaw said. Discover the motive and the murderer is on their way to the hangman's trapdoor."

He turned his chair to catch the sunlight from the window, aware that the suspects were left with his portly profile. (He had always thought that he had the look of a J.B. Priestley.) "It's generally less than three days after the submission of final arguments to the Home Secretary and, by that time you - one of you - will have spent several weeks in the condemned cell with a warder for company. A warder and a Bible, of course. On the morning of the topping-off, the procedure is speedy. Usually less than twenty seconds, I'm told, although the one I witnessed was a messy affair and took much longer. Not minutes, please don't think that, but considerably more than twenty seconds. I'm frequently amused by pictures showing the rope rising up from the back of the head. It's not at all like that. They skew it to one side. It makes a cleaner break in the neck. Do you know, you're left hanging for ninety minutes before they do an autopsy? Over long, don't you think?"

Margot Worth was the first to break into tears. "You must stop this!" She buried her head in her hands, then let her fingers draw down her face until she could see again. "Haven't we all been through enough? Whoever did this, for God's sake own up and let the rest of us go home."

But Storey wouldn't allow them to think that only one was guilty and the rest were innocent. "Home? Only after you have all been charged with licentious publication," he said. "Whatever the outcome, we still have the matter of the photographs." He allowed the thought to weigh in the room.

Now, to test them. "Tell me, who thought of the grey haired tortoise? It wasn't Skelton. That man hasn't the imagination for it. Really, I'd like to know."

Jean Paul had fixed his gaze on a corner of the ceiling and responded to Storey's question by sucking loudly through his teeth.

"I think it was you, Mrs Worth. Sergeant Horndean has done some research for me."

"I played no part in that hoax!"

"He could find only one reference to a grey haired tortoise and that was in an ancient anatomy book."

Miss Langworthy shifted to the edge of her seat and chewed her lips. She tried, but she couldn't keep her words in. "Why are you doing this? If you know who did it, arrest them and be done with it."

Because, Storey said in his head, I want each of you to dread the prospect of my getting it wrong. I want you to be scared that I'll make a mistake and send the wrong person to the gallows. This will be all over before lunchtime but nonetheless I want you all to taste that fear.

"I won't listen." Langworthy jerked her head back.

"Following the murder of Edith Winterton, Cadet Holden saw the waitress Julie run out of the Red Rose restaurant. Mr Williams had threatened to leave her alone with you, Jean Paul, and she was frightened out of her mind. Why? I think there can only be one reason. I think she had resisted your demands that she should take part in your filthy circle. Now, she was scared that she would be killed if she refused. Am I wrong?"

"Ask her on the end," Dusty snarled, meaning Langworthy.

"Of course, I'm not wrong. The truth is that you were a divided party when it came to Julie's recruitment. On the night Edith Winterton died, she intended to call on you, Miss Langworthy, hoping to win you over. For or against? This murder only makes sense if Edith wanted Jean Paul to get his way. One of you was determined that Edith's pleading wouldn't succeed and you killed her. Now, is that motive enough for murder? Let's consider the point."

He turned back to his desk and fumbled his pipe between his fingers. "I don't think that Edith would have been murdered in order to guarantee Julie's involvement. Hardly necessary, surely? But, if one of you wanted to protect the girl? To get the others off her back? To save her? Yes, I think here is our motive. As Mr Evanshaw would tell us, we are well on our path to the hangman's cell."

"But what about Dominic's murder?" said the man's widow. "You need to prove that as well."

"Any one of you could have killed Mr Worth. Jean Paul knew how to get into this police station without being seen - for years, he had been hauling books up and down the canteen waste chute - and he could have shared his secret passage with any of you. You see, Worth was the real danger to you all. He was never part of your circle but knew all of its goings on and he was the one who couldn't be trusted. Whoever killed Edith

Winterton had to kill Dominic Worth before he spoke out." He pressed his knuckles into his desktop. "Who was protecting Red Rose Julie?"

Storey stood up. "I think the murder of Captain Forsyte is the key to this affair."

"No." Dusty Ainsworth was shaking her head, trying to catch the faces of the conspirators and pleading with the detective. "He was nothing to do with us."

"He was close to you, Dusty, and he'd already given part of his evidence to Sergeant Faulkner. But he had more to tell. He knew, didn't he? He knew your whereabouts at the times of the murders, or had you made some slip that made no sense to him?"

"No."

"But only two people were seen at his house that morning. Jean Paul and Dusty Ainsworth."

"No. You must listen to what the doctor said."

"Oh, you wanted us to think that only a stranger would make the mistake with his gloved hand, just as you wanted us to believe the date and time in this photograph."

"They were going to ruin her," she snarled viciously. "Once they got hold of her. The little wretch came to me for help." She tossed her head. "Help! Precious little in your damn souls. Damn you!"

Langworthy threw her head back and laughed. "Listen to this! My God, Inspector Storey, our little town is in for quite a scandal."

He said quietly, "Dusty Ainsworth, you killed Edith Winterton, Dominic Worth and the game-handed Captain Forsyte," but she was on her feet and shouting.

"I'll talk. I'll get you all into trouble!"

Jean Paul and Langworthy stayed stoic. Margot Worth fell forward in sobs.

"Get them all out here, Faulkner. They foul the air."

It was close to midnight when Inspector and Mrs Storey walked down High Street. They wanted to enjoy the night air before calling a taxi. He had suggested heading for the town bridge with the option of changing their minds. Janine was wearing her special frock and attractive stockings and felt, at last, that she had her man to herself. They would talk about the case, of course they would; there was much that he needed to say and much that she wanted to learn, but they would be talking about something that was already in the past and she could steer him away from those troubled silences that dogged his work.

"The town will remember these murders for a long time," he said as he stroked his fingers over her loosely held hand. He remembered how he used to be frightened of crushing her knuckles. He had been nervous of her flying away in those early days. He used to call her his petty moineau. (He had always been worried that it meant small change but she seemed to like it.)

"Because of the sex, you mean?"

"And the reasons behind the resignation of a Chief Constable. It's the sort of case that people can feel guilty about. There'll be an unspoken worry that they shouldn't have let it happen. A case like this reaches beyond the conspirators."

She leaned closer to him as they walked. Any closer and she'll be asking to wrap herself in my coat, he thought.

He gave a short laugh. "It all started with a joke."

"No, Brian. It started with a young girl who wanted to keep herself clean. Hold me, honey. Put your arm around me. It's nice walking but it's cold."

As they passed through the town square, where three motor coaches were moored for the night, the cathedral clock turned the page of a new day. The strident bell of a police car reached them from another part of town. That's against the rules after nine o'clock, he thought idly.

"There's something of Joe Venuti in that fiddle player."

"My husband? Listening to jazz?"

"No." He confessed, "I cribbed it from Horndean. They are an interesting couple. We should nurture their friendship," which prompted Janine's silly sparrow-like giggle.

He stopped. "What's so funny?"

"I'm trying to picture you listening to jazz and calling Sergeant Horndean by his first name."

He grunted and walked on. "Unlikely. I'm not good with people. Any news yet?"

"Don't be silly. It's far too early to tell."

They reached the bridge and leaned over to look into the dark water.

"You did well, Brian."

"Yes," he said as if it really didn't matter. "Very likely."